From its spark-filled beg
conclusion, *No Place Like Home*
of faith-filled romance will er
Anguish reminding us that hon
family, especially when we learn to bloom wherever we're
planted.

— CANDEE FICK, AUTHOR OF THE
WARDROBE SERIES

Once again, Amy Anguish has given the reader a sweet love story and highly believable characters. I don't know of many Christians who haven't gone through periods of doubt, and in this novel, the theme of putting your trust in God plays out on many levels. I could see myself in more than one character. If you like sweet romance, all-too-human characters, and a few surprises, read *No Place Like Home*. I was encouraged, personally. You will be, too.

— REGINA RUDD MERRICK, AUTHOR OF
THE SOUTHERN BREEZE SERIES

No Place
LIKE HOME

AMY R. ANGUISH

Scrivenings
PRESS
Quench your thirst for story.
www.ScriveningsPress.com

Even though they have all passed on, I was blessed with amazing Christian women who took me under their wings through my growing up years, and helped me feel loved even in the hard times. This book goes out to Ms. Olga, Ms. Violet, Ms. Kathleen (Sparky), and Ms. Earline. Their efforts aided me in remembering that even though the church is made of up of imperfect people, there will always be ones who care and want to help you be your best.

Copyright © 2021 by Amy Anguish

Published by Scrivenings Press LLC
15 Lucky Lane
Morrilton, Arkansas 72110
https://ScriveningsPress.com

Printed in the United States of America

All rights reserved. No part of this publication may be reproduced, stored in a retrieval system, or transmitted in any form or by any means—for example, electronic, photocopy and recording— without the prior written permission of the publisher. The only exception is brief quotations in printed reviews.

Paperback ISBN 978-1-64917-167-2

eBook ISBN 978-1-64917-168-9

Library of Congress Control Number: 2021948009

Editors: Shannon Vannatter and K. Banks

Cover by Linda Fulkerson, bookmarketinggraphics.com

All characters are fictional, and any resemblance to real people, either factual or historical, is purely coincidental.

Scripture taken from the New King James Version®. Copyright © 1982 by Thomas Nelson. Used by permission. All rights reserved.

1

"You need to let them know."

Adrian's answering huff echoed through the phone. Danielle had always considered herself the big sister despite being only a few minutes older.

"I'm serious." Danielle continued. "It's not fair for you to be the closest you've been in years and not at least make some effort to see them."

"That's easy for you to say. You get along with our parents." Adrian leaned too close to the window, and her breath clouded up the glass. She wiped away the moisture with the back of her hand. Fog swept over the land outside, creeping up from Lake Michigan and spreading out into the city. Not like the 'cat feet' the poet had claimed years before. More like a floating wave. Or an army of ghosts.

The park across the street was so thick with it, Adrian could hardly make out any of the strange metal statues or the new buds on the trees just starting to bloom. Spring seemed to come later here than in the places she grew up. 'Most everything would be green in the south now.

"Adie, seriously." Danielle's chiding cut through Adrian's mental fog. "It takes two to have a relationship. If you'd quit approaching them with hackles raised and actually attempt keeping the peace, you know things would go easier. But it's like you come with a chip on your shoulder the size of Minnesota every time you visit them. Not that you visit that much."

"Minnesota?"

"It was the first state to pop into my head." Danielle's voice carried that *Don't mess with me—you know what I meant* tone only a mother could pull off.

Adrian ignored it. "Why would Minnesota be the first state to pop in your head?"

"I don't know. Quit trying to change the subject."

Adrian glanced at her watch. Saved by the bell. "Look, Danielle, as much as I love a good sparring match first thing in the morning, I have a meeting soon. I'll keep your advice in mind."

"Adrian—"

"Love you, too, sis. I'll talk to you later." Adrian ended the call before her sister could reprimand her more. Deep down, she knew Danielle was right. The awkwardness between her and their parents was mostly her fault. After all, she was the one who quit trusting God eight years before. That was more than a little hard for her preacher dad to swallow.

She stepped back from the window and took a sip of her coffee. This was her last day in Chicago. The winter had passed more quickly than she'd expected, and her time working here to train Premium Healthcare of Illinois employees was done.

They had most of the ins and outs of the computer program figured out now and could handle the rest through basic tech support online and over the phone. She would run by their office one last time later this morning and then pack her few things to be ready to head south tomorrow. She glanced at her watch—ten minutes.

Video meetings didn't require her to change out of her yoga pants. That could wait. But she did run a brush through her hair and throw on a decent shirt. She hummed "Oh, What a

Beautiful Mornin'" as she pulled out her laptop and checked emails one more time before the call would begin.

The circle went round and round on her screen as she waited for someone else to log in for the conference. Her coffee was getting cold, but it was a risk leaving to warm it up this close to the meeting time.

The screen flickered, and then Brad's face appeared in one of the boxes. His hair had a bit more silver around the temples now than it had when she first started working with him, although he couldn't be more than ten years her senior. Did he look more harried than usual?

He leaned forward to adjust something on his computer and straightened a few papers before realizing she was there and watching him. "I should have known you'd already be on here."

"You know me." Adrian crisscrossed her legs under the table and grinned. "I can't stand being late, so I'm always early."

This was her fifth year working for MidUSLogIn Inc. The last four she'd handled a big chunk of their out-of-town training. Among other places, she'd spent time in Kansas City, Louisville, Springfield, and Indianapolis, as well as the four months finishing up in Chicago now. Since she'd helped develop the software, she was good at her job of staying to work one on one with each company to make sure they could use the software properly.

This morning Adrian would chat with her boss and the head of the IT department at the next place she'd be heading. In a month she'd be in Memphis, Tennessee, the farthest south she'd ventured since starting with MLI. When Brad Donahue and Michael Laramie had started MidUSLogIn Inc., they'd hoped to spread to two or three states. This would make six.

"Gray should be on here any minute now. I just got off the phone with him." Brad tapped his pen on the papers he was studying. "He had to do one quick thing before he joined us. You ready to head south again?"

"I don't know. It's starting to warm up here in the Windy City."

He glanced up as if to see if she was teasing. She was.

"Chicago has been one of my favorite cities to live in so far, Brad, but you know I'll go anywhere you need me. I don't have any roots or plans to put any down."

He shook his head. "I don't know how you do it. I can't sleep well when I'm gone for one night. You stay at these places for months at a time, never sleep in your own bed, hardly get to see your family."

"It's not so bad. The extended-stay hotels I end up in are really nice, I keep my movies and books with me, and my family and I don't always get along anyway. Plus, I get to see all these different places."

"You might get along better with your family if you saw them more often."

Before she could reply, the left side of her screen flickered and another man joined their video conference. For someone named Gray, he didn't remind her of the color at all. His blond hair waved a bit across the top of his head, his blue eyes crinkled at the edges, and his smile was like a ray of sunshine. Usually, Adrian didn't pay much attention to men, but this one made her breath catch a little. She mentally shook herself and focused back on the task at hand.

"Adrian Stewart, this is Grayson Roberts. He's the head of the IT department at Healthcare for All in Memphis. You'll be working closely with him the first few weeks while you make sure the software is set up and ready to go. After that, he'll help you get everyone else trained."

She gave a little wave at the screen and smiled. "Hi."

He nodded his head and grinned even bigger than he had been. "How are you?"

It was a typical southern greeting, one she hadn't heard much in the last few months. Chicago was nice, but it had nothing on the South when it came to charm. She knew the question didn't need a real answer—it was just what people said when they met someone. But it was still nice to hear.

"We should be good to go on our end." Brad flipped through his papers again. "Gray, I think you gave me the last bit of information we needed this morning, so we can get those final few drop boxes installed in the software. Adrian will stop by here in the next day or so to go over everything and make sure she knows how it's set up for you guys. Then she's getting a much-needed vacation for a couple weeks before she heads your way."

Adrian hid her scowl. She hadn't wanted the vacation, but Brad threatened to quit paying her if she didn't take some time off. Not that she had any idea what she'd do with that time. She wasn't good at doing nothing.

"That'll be great," Gray said. His voice was deep. If he were singing, he'd be a bass. "Our aim is to get this rolled out at the beginning of July, so that should give us around a month to get it set up, installed, and everyone trained on the basic stuff. That's reasonable, right?"

"How big is your company again?" Adrian asked, glancing through the information sheet Brad had faxed her last week.

"We have about five hundred employees who will use it to clock in and out and about fifty-five in the offices using the program to work with the clients and monitor payroll."

"We'll do our best, but that might be pushing it a bit to get everyone trained. I usually want at least three or four days to work with the office staff on basics, then at least another week to see what issues and questions arise." Adrian's finger traced the line that said Healthcare for All had five locations. "Are we combining training for all the locations, or will we be doing separate trainings at each one?"

"We're combining trainings with two sessions each." Gray's eyes never left the screen.

"That should be more than doable, then." Brad tapped a pen against his desk. "Adrian is the best."

She shook her head. "I don't know about that, but I'll do my best to make it happen if we can. Cross your fingers we don't run into any complications."

Their software helped businesses monitor their staff members by giving them a more accurate way to log time worked. Companies who provided home health services were attracted to the ability the software gave their employees to use their phones to clock in and out, even from clients' homes.

It was much more efficient than logging hours on a piece of paper. It also allowed the workplaces to keep track of information to better serve their clients and make sure each worker got paid for the right hours. But more employees using it made it more likely something could go wrong.

"I'll let my boss know your concerns and see what she thinks, but if Brad thinks we can do it in this timeframe, we'll probably stick with the original plan." Gray leaned back in his chair. "And I'll pray for smooth transitions."

Adrian chose not to comment on that. She and God were not on speaking terms. Hadn't been for years. If Grayson was going to pray about the trainings she was about to do, she'd better expect complications and problems.

"Anything Adrian needs to know before she arrives in a few weeks?" Brad asked.

Gray sat forward again. "Not that I can think of. I sent her my contact information so she can call if she thinks of anything."

"I got the email about the extended-stay hotel I've booked, too, so I'm good to go there. I'll call you or email if I think of anything between now and June." Adrian set aside the papers and finally looked back at the handsome man on her screen.

Gray gave her a smile. "Sounds like we're set. I'm looking forward to meeting you in person."

"Sounds good. I'll see you in June."

"And I'll see you in a few days, Adrian," Brad said.

They all ended the video conference at the same time, and she shook her head. What was it about Grayson Roberts that had her so kerfuffled? She couldn't remember the last time a man's appearance had made her catch her breath.

She stood up and refreshed her coffee. Looking out the window, she was almost surprised to see how foggy it still was. Somehow Gray had made it seem a lot sunnier. She stirred some more creamer into her mug. *Get it together, girl. You're working with him, not dating him. AND he's obviously a Christian. You don't want to go back down that road.*

Speaking of Christians, Danielle was right, loath as she was to admit it. She should probably call her parents. If they found out she had time off and didn't come see them for at least a couple of days, they'd be beyond hurt. She dreaded visiting them because of the disappointment in their faces each time they realized she still wasn't going back to church. After all, how bad did it look when the preacher's own daughter wouldn't join him there?

She put it off several more minutes by packing up a few things. Since she lived in an extended-stay hotel whenever she did trainings, she didn't need much. But she liked to have some personal items—her entire collection of old musicals to watch, a few of her favorite books, a couple of pictures of family.

Gently placing each frame in the top of the box of books, she wrapped them up with some scarves for protection. Tonight, before bed, she could move the clothes from the drawers to the suitcases. That just left a few favorite mugs and her personal coffee maker that went with her even though most hotels had one in each room. Hers was faster and brewed it stronger, two things she needed first thing in the morning.

Moving a box packed full of her movies, she sat down on the couch and clicked the button to call her mom. Better get this over with so she wouldn't have to think about it later.

"Adrian?" Her mom answered on the second ring. "Everything okay, honey?"

Every time Adrian called over the last few years, her mom had answered the phone almost exactly the same way. Her voice was always careful, expectant, hopeful. Adrian stifled a sigh. She hated having made her mom sound like that whenever she talked to her. She didn't want their relationship to be strained, but she couldn't find a way to fix it either.

"It's fine, Mom. It's my last full day in Chicago. I'm just finishing up a few things today, then headed back to St. Louis tomorrow."

"You've been up there a while now, right?" Adrian could hear her mom doing dishes as she talked on the phone.

"About four months. Winter is definitely colder up here." This was her life. She'd rather talk to her mom about the weather than about coming to visit. She bit her lip. "I have some vacation time coming up."

"Oh?" That one word from her mom came out with so much hope.

Adrian blinked and swallowed against the tightening in her throat. "Thought I might swing down and see you guys for a few days. If that's all right."

"You know it is. We'll have to let Danny know you're coming. I'm sure she'd like to come over and see you while you're here. It's been a while."

Adrian picked at a spot on the sofa. "It will be good to see her too." She didn't dare let her mom know she'd been on the phone with Danielle earlier. Even though they looked exactly alike, they were almost complete opposites. But Adrian kept up with Danny better than she kept up with her parents. There was less friction between them, and Adrian could be herself with her sister.

"Do you know what days exactly?" her mom asked.

"I'm not sure yet. I'll see how long they need me at the office in St. Louis before I figure out my exact dates off. I know I need to be in Memphis by June first."

"You're going to Memphis?"

"That's my next job. I'll be there a couple months, probably —maybe a little longer." Adrian had kept that tidbit to herself until now too. Memphis was only about two and a half hours from the small north Arkansas town where her parents lived, close enough they might expect to see her more.

"Just across the river from us."

"And a few hours." Adrian stood up and paced back to the window. The early morning fog was starting to dissipate, and she could make out the strange metal legs of the statues across the street. "I'll be pretty busy, though. This company wants everything running a month from when I get there."

"Still, it will be nice to think of you so close. You know, if you decide to come for your vacation days around the twenty-second, we're having an area-wide gospel singing. It would be nice to hear your voice again."

"You know I love singing, Mom. But I love singing songs from musicals or the radio. Not ..." Adrian's voice trailed off. "I don't know exactly what dates I'll come, but I'll let you know next week, okay?"

"Of course, Adrian." Her mom's voice sounded a little more strained than it had a few minutes before. "You know we'll love to have you whenever you come. You be safe driving home tomorrow, okay?"

Adrian took her coffee cup and set it in the sink. "I always am."

"I'll be praying for you."

You always do, Mom. For all the good it does ...

2

Grayson Roberts had determined a long time ago never to date a non-Christian. After all, his parents' lack of a faith in God ruined the first fifteen years of his life. And the way Adrian Stewarts's eyes shifted when he mentioned praying for their success, he had a feeling she didn't share his beliefs.

So why couldn't he shake her from his thoughts this afternoon? They hadn't even spoken that long and never in person. All he had was a first impression through a computer screen.

"Gray?" Diane, the head of accounting, stood in his doorway. "Payroll is messing up again." Her hair frizzed around the edge of her braid, as if she'd clasped her head in her hands multiple times that day.

"Okay. Let's see what's going on." Gray followed her back to her workspace and clicked through the multiple screens open on her computer.

"How long before we get the new software?" Diane sank into a chair next to him.

"Just a few more weeks. First of June, we start training." He clicked on a couple of different boxes and ran the program again.

Maybe this time, all the information needed would pull correctly. Otherwise, it would be a late night.

"It can't come soon enough. This program is so outdated it seems to grow problems by the hour." Diane waved at the screen. "This new one better work more efficiently."

"I've heard nothing but good reports about it." Gray pressed his hands together, sending up a quick prayer that all would be right when he opened the report back up. "Ta-da. How's this look?"

Diane peered over his shoulder, motioning him to scroll through the data so she could see more. "Yes. Yes, it looks like it's at least mostly there this time. Much closer anyway."

"Good."

"Any hope of moving up the start date on the new program?"

"I don't know. It sounds like the training lady is due some vacation time before she heads our way. I can't imagine taking that away from her. Plus, I don't think we're quite set up to start it here, anyway. They're adding a few things we requested. And we need to work out everyone's schedules so they can sit through her sessions while others cover their workload. It's a lot to organize, and we still have a few hoops to jump through."

"I may go talk to Riley about it anyway. Every week I fear we're tempting fate to keep using this antiquated software." Diane pulled the report off the printer and waved it at him. "It's at least worth looking into."

"Let me know what she says." Gray saluted her as he walked back downstairs to the IT department.

The thought of seeing Adrian sooner set a battle waging within him. Sure, he was excited about getting his hands on a program to make payroll and client data easier to work with. But, more than that, he wanted to see if the woman on the computer screen was as intriguing in real life as she was hundreds of miles away.

And that was probably the stupidest thing to focus on. Especially if she didn't believe in prayer. But those few minutes online together were enough to leave a lasting image of her eyes and smile in his head whenever he stopped to daydream for a minute. Enough to make him hope Vice President Riley would agree with Diane and try to move up their start date.

BRAD MADE sure Adrian didn't work many more days. The next Tuesday, she found herself driving south on I-55 toward Arkansas. Her parents had moved to a small town northeast of Little Rock the year before her senior year of high school. This was the longest they'd lived anywhere.

Growing up, her family ended up moving about every three years. She'd lived in one town for six, but just like every other place, it didn't last.

Her fingers tightened on the steering wheel until her knuckles turned white. *Stop thinking about it. That part of your life is over.* She pried a hand off the wheel to reach over and turn up the volume on the radio. Maybe Taylor Swift could drown out her past, even while she headed towards it at seventy miles an hour.

It wasn't that she didn't love her family. They just didn't understand. Yes, her dad chose preaching as his profession and couldn't turn his back on it, but why did it seem like his job was more important than his daughter? She followed the signs through southern Missouri and into Arkansas. Just another hour and a half. Still time to turn around ...

She straightened her shoulders and readjusted her hands on the steering wheel. No. She'd keep going. There was nothing for her to do back at her apartment in St. Louis this week. A road sign noted the number of miles to Memphis, but she'd get off before then. The towns her father chose to work in were never big enough to be close to an interstate. She saw her exit, took a deep breath, and pointed her car west.

At least Danielle promised she'd be there with the kids tonight. Adrian's sister lived in Little Rock with her husband but spent quite a bit of time with their parents. Adrian wasn't sure if it was to make up for the fact that Adrian spent almost no time with them or if she just really liked being there.

To distract herself from her anxiety, Adrian focused on everything she'd need to do when she started the job in Memphis. Gray had been in touch, saying everything was going great and that he looked forward to working with her. She still couldn't put her finger on precisely what it was about him that made her feel so fluttery inside.

She'd seen handsome men before and not reacted this way. And it wasn't like she'd seen him more than the short video conference the other day, so she didn't know much about him at all. But still ... he hit a vibe inside her that made her yearn to get to Memphis faster.

She checked the rearview mirror but couldn't see the road sign for Memphis anymore. *I'm supposed to be thinking about work, not coworkers.* She laughed at herself. *Actually, I'm not supposed to be thinking about anything work-related. I'm on vacation.*

The house the church provided for her parents was a simple, one-story brick ranch with three bedrooms and a den. Her mom was working in the front flower bed when Adrian pulled her Honda into the drive.

No one could deny Adrian and Danielle were related to their mom—all had the same heart-shaped face, hair color, and hazel eyes. As Mom stood up and brushed dirt from her knees, Adrian imagined she was looking at herself in twenty years. If that were true, she'd age well. Beth Stewart still appeared younger than her fifty years, although Adrian noticed a few more grays mixed in with the brown hair. Her mom's face lit up as Adrian got out of the car.

Even after everything that had happened the last few years, her mom's hug was warm and comforting. Some of the tension seeped from Adrian's shoulders as her mom's arms squeezed her close. She breathed in the scent of sunshine and soil that took her back to years of helping her mom work in gardens they might have to leave before harvest. Adrian shook that sad thought away and reveled in the hug.

"How are you, sweetie?" Her mom pulled away enough to look Adrian in the eyes.

"I'm fine." Adrian turned and grabbed her bag and pillow out of the car. She was only planning to stay a few days. Three seemed to be the maximum number she could be with her family before things got too heated, so she usually left after two and a half.

"Not sure what I'm supposed to do with time off, though. Brad insisted I take a week of vacation. He said I had too many vacation days saved up, and he was tired of seeing them go to waste."

"Everyone needs a break now and then."

"I guess." Adrian followed her mother into the house. The cinnamon scent of her favorite cookies filled the air, and she breathed in deeply—snickerdoodles. All was as it had been the last time she visited. Old school pictures on the wall of the living room, dining table half-piled with projects her mom was working on for one organization or another, several pairs of reading glasses lay waiting, each assigned to its own piece of furniture.

Her mom waved toward the hall. "Your room is ready as always. Lay your stuff down and come have a cookie."

Though Adrian pleaded not to move here since it was right before her senior year of high school, she'd ended up here for a year. Still, this had never felt like home. Down the hall, the room remained locked in time, with her old twin bed, the cheval mirror she'd begged for one Christmas, her high school diploma and graduation picture in matching frames on the wall. Her various yearbooks sat on a shelf along with other high school mementos she'd left behind.

She ran a finger around the glass she got at prom, full of the petals from her corsage. She hadn't even wanted to go, but Danielle insisted. Wandering back to the kitchen, she sat on a stool at the bar. Her mom had a plate of cookies and a mug of coffee ready for her. She took a bite of a still-warm snickerdoodle and sighed. No one could get them as soft and chewy as her mom.

"It's a shame you won't be here through Friday." Her mom took a sip of coffee. "The singing is this weekend."

"Mom—"

Her mom held her hands up as if to surrender. "I know. I won't push it. But a mother can miss hearing her daughter sing, can't she?"

"I'm sure Danny and her family will come."

"Of course. But, oh, to hear you two sing together again ... that would be a bit of heaven on earth."

"Maybe we can do some show tunes together tonight." Adrian took another bite of cookie, trying to figure out how to change the subject. She was not going to a gospel singing. There was no need for her to sing songs she didn't mean to a God who didn't love her.

"You know that's not the kind of song I love to hear you sing."

The backdoor opened before Adrian could reply. Her father walked into the kitchen, his focus on the mail in his hand. He glanced up and gave her a smile that didn't quite reach all the way to his eyes, as if he wanted to test the waters before he gave her a full-hearted one. How sad that she got a warmer smile from Gray Roberts on a video conference than from her parents.

"Hello, A." Her dad always referred to his daughters by their first initials. He said he did it because he couldn't really come up with a nickname for Adrian and didn't think it was fair for Danny to have one when she didn't.

Adrian stood and side-hugged him. "Hey, Dad."

"I was just trying to talk Adrian into staying for the singing this Friday." Her mom stood and gave him a light peck on the lips.

"I didn't pack much for my visit. I still need to go back to St. Louis and get my stuff before I can head to Memphis next week." Adrian didn't offer an apology. She wasn't sorry she'd miss the singing. She'd planned it that way.

"The girl is busy, Beth. Maybe another time." Her father snitched a cookie and walked out to the den.

Her mom sat back down at the counter. "Your sister should be here in a little while."

Adrian nodded. "I talked to her the other day. She said the kids are excited to see me."

"You won't believe how much they've grown. Timmy is loving preschool, thinks he's big man on campus. And Seth is so sweet and loving. No terrible twos for him. He has lots of snuggles for his Nana."

"Sounds a lot like his mama." Adrian had been the wilder one of the twins. It had never surprised her that Danny got married and settled down to raise a family right out of college.

"They're both sweet boys." Her mom picked at a spot on the counter with her thumbnail.

"Want some help with your weeding? I think I interrupted you."

"Sure. That would be nice."

She followed her mom outside, and they knelt side by side in the warm dirt, cleaning out her mother's flower garden. The sun was warm on her back, and Adrian pushed up her sleeves. She'd forgotten that Arkansas warmed up faster than St. Louis and Chicago. Neither woman spoke, just worked in silence.

In high school, Adrian never had any trouble talking to her parents. Now it seemed like every conversation led to a road one or the other of them didn't want to go down. If this was how the next two days would be, Adrian might never take a vacation again.

3

"How much does this remind you of sleeping at Grandma's house growing up?" Danielle and Adrian lay in the full-sized bed in Danielle's old room late that night. The boys were tucked away in *Aunt Adie's room* across the hall, and since Danny's husband, Phil, was still in Little Rock, Adrian crawled in with her sister.

"I don't know. It seems like there was more fighting over the covers when we were growing up and had to share a bed."

"Want me to tug them all to my side?" Danielle gave a pull.

"You probably will before the night is over anyway."

Danny's pillow hit Adrian's face with a *plop*.

Adrian threw it back at her. "Will you ever grow up?"

"You mean like you did?"

"What does that mean?" Adrian propped herself up on one elbow.

Danny rolled over onto her back and let out a sigh. "I don't know, Adie. You know I love you, but I hate seeing how much Mom and Dad worry about you."

"I don't know why they worry so much. I'm doing fine. I have a great job that I love, a nice little apartment in St. Louis, enough money to live on with a bit to put back for retirement. I get to see lots of new places."

Granted, her apartment was more of a storage unit for her bed and dresser. She didn't have many pieces of furniture since she lived away most of the time. Why spend money on things that would just sit and collect dust while she was gone?

"And they're happy for you for all those things, but you know what they're really upset about."

Adrian flopped back onto her pillow. "Why can't I have one visit without everyone harping on me?"

"No one is harping on you."

"Mom feels the need to practically break down and cry just because I won't come to the singing on Friday." Adrian ticked everyone off on her fingers. "Dad barely acknowledges my existence. You're the only one who treats me like a normal person, and even you're pushing it tonight."

"Thanks a lot, kid." Danny had always teased Adrian about being twenty minutes younger.

"You know what I mean."

"Mom thinks if she doesn't say *something* when she talks with you, she hasn't at least tried to make things better. Dad hopes not talking about the issue will ease the tension and make things easier. Instead, it just makes it worse. They don't understand why you left the church." Danny rolled over to face Adrian. "I'm not completely sure either."

"I don't see the point in going to a worship service for a God who doesn't love me."

"Adrian ..."

"Stop, Danny. What has God ever done for me?" Adrian held up a hand before her sister could answer. "No. I don't want to talk about it anymore."

Danielle was silent for a moment. "I just have this feeling that if God wants you back, you won't have a choice. And there's a lot of people praying for that to happen."

"What about free will? Didn't Dad always preach about how we're free to make our own decisions?"

"*That's* what you remember about Dad's sermons?" Danielle let out a half-hearted laugh. "Good grief. No wonder your faith is so messed up."

Adrian sent her sister a dirty look even though the room was dark. Evidently, her silence clued Danny into the fact she truly didn't want to talk about this anymore. They were quiet for a few moments, listening to the grandmother clock in the living room as it chimed out midnight, their dad snoring down the hall, a lone train whistle blowing a few blocks down the street.

"The boys had a good time with you tonight." Danielle broke the silence.

Adrian grinned in the dark. "They're the only ones in the family who just love me no matter what."

"Kids are like that."

"Mom really seems to love being a nana. You going to give her any more grandbabies, or are you done?"

Danielle shoved Adrian playfully. "I think it's about time you joined in and gave her a grandbaby. Anyone looking good for husband material?"

"I don't have time for a husband. I'm constantly traveling, living out of a suitcase, and at an office. When would I have time to meet a guy?" Adrian tried to squelch the image of Grayson Roberts that popped into her head.

"What was that look for?"

"We're in the dark. You can't see the look on my face."

"The moon is shining right on your face, Adrian. I can see it just fine." Danielle propped up on her elbow. "And that face said you were keeping something from me."

"You're crazy. It's late. Go to sleep."

"Ha!" Danielle half tackled her. "I've known you for almost twenty-six years. You're keeping something from me, and I bet it's about a guy. Spill it!"

Adrian pushed against her sister but couldn't get a good angle to move her much because of the soft mattress. "Get off!"

"Not until you spill."

"There's nothing to spill." Adrian huffed.

"I will get this out of you."

Adrian squirmed again. "There's nothing to get out. Get off of me!"

Across the hall, one of the boys cried out in his sleep. Danielle sat up a bit, and Adrian took advantage of the moment to get out from under her sister. When they didn't hear anything else, Danielle laid back down.

"But things are good?"

"I told you they were. I loved my stint in Chicago. I think if I weren't working out of St. Louis, I'd probably want to live there. The buildings are gorgeous, the lake is amazing—you can't even begin to see the other side of it, so it feels like an ocean—and I'm not sure I'll ever like thin-crust pizza again."

"I still think you're hiding something from me."

Adrian rolled over with her back to her sister. "That's your prerogative. Get some sleep. Those boys get up way too early."

"I'm hoping maybe Mom will keep them occupied until we get up."

"That's a sweet dream." Adrian listened as her sister's breathing evened out and got a slight whiffle, though not even a shadow of the grizzly-sized snores coming from their father down the hall. Even though she hadn't wanted to come, she was glad she had if for no other reason than the time with her sister. If only things weren't so awkward with her parents.

ADRIAN'S PHONE rang at breakfast the next morning. "Hey Brad, what's going on?"

"Sorry to bug you during your vacation, but we may have a problem."

She stepped out into the carport, where her conversation wouldn't interrupt anyone's waffle eating. "Oh?"

"Healthcare for All may need you sooner than the end of next week. Gray's boss is thinking we haven't allotted enough time to get everyone trained correctly. I don't want you to have to cut your vacation short—"

"Don't worry about me. Do they want me this week?"

"The end of the week is what he said. That way, you and Gray can get a few things hammered out and then start training next week."

Adrian glanced up to see her mom at the window. She grinned at her even as she knew she was about to break her heart a little more. "I'll head home today to grab my things and can be in Memphis late Thursday."

"Friday is fine. Don't push yourself too hard. And we'll make sure you get the rest of your vacation once you're finished with this training."

"Sure. That's not a problem. I'll swing by the office either this afternoon or tomorrow." Adrian looked out on her mother's perfect yard. Adrian hadn't inherited her mother's green thumb —partly because she never stayed in one place long enough to give the plants the care they needed. Too hard to water plants from three hundred miles away.

It was peaceful out here, and she lingered a few minutes to breathe in the honeysuckle growing on the fence. Straightening her shoulders, she turned to go back in. She'd finish her waffle, say goodbye to everyone, and head back north. At least now she had a better reason to give her mom for not going to the singing on Friday.

"GRAY!" Riley called from her office as Gray walked down the hallway.

He spun on his heel and raised an eyebrow. "Yes?"

"You're ready for the MidUSLogIn girl, right? Because she'll be here tomorrow."

"You got it moved up?" Gray leaned against the doorframe.

"I did."

"Great. We should be ready, but I'll double-check things when I get back downstairs. Where were you thinking her workspace would be?"

"Since she's only temporary and basically working with you the whole time, I figured that extra table in your office would be best for her landing spot. I mean, most of her time at first will be in the conference room doing training, right?" Riley barely glanced up from some notes she was sorting through.

Gray rubbed the back of his neck. "Ri-ight."

"Uh, oh." Riley glanced his way. "How deep is the pile this time?"

"I'll make sure it's useable." He drummed his fingers on the wall. "Anything else?"

"No. That's it for now. Let me know if you need anything else before she gets here."

"Will do."

His office. The tiny little corner of the basement he called his own was barely big enough to turn around in. And they would have to share it. Considering his warning to himself about maintaining his distance from Adrian Stewart until he determined her stance on God, this could get interesting.

The sight of his piles of paperwork and paraphernalia stopped him as he entered his domain. Mama would kill him if she knew he let it get this bad. When had it happened?

He scooped up the top layer and shuffled through a few things, filing some in the trash and moving a few more to the top of the filing cabinet for later. His phone pulled him away from the task. Two help tickets later, it was almost the end of the day, and most of the mess remained. He let out a sigh. He'd have to tackle it first thing in the morning. It definitely wasn't happening now.

One more walkthrough of the conference room and he had everything else as ready as he could. Now to prepare the wall around his heart and make sure those hazel eyes didn't penetrate it until he was ready. Shouldn't be too hard. Especially knowing she wasn't supposed to be here that long.

4

Driving through Missouri and Arkansas, a person got used to how flat things were. A few gently rolling hills broke up the evenness only slightly. Field after field of cotton, rice, and wheat grew in green patterned rows, making the landscape look like a giant crazy quilt.

Adrian's car bumped along Interstate 55 as she drove south on Friday. Her windshield wipers swished through the drizzle and left a grimy streak at the edge of her window.

This was her tenth training. After she'd gone through the first one, four years before, she hadn't been nervous as she headed into any of the others. Butterflies were keeping her tummy on edge this afternoon, though, and she wasn't sure why. She leaned her head to the side to stretch out a crick in her neck and hummed along with the radio.

West Memphis appeared almost out of nowhere, and she followed the road signs as she maneuvered through the construction. A few turns and she could see the bridge. Almost there.

The Pyramid stood sentinel to her left, up at the I-40 bridge. Following I-55, she took the south loop to her hotel. She checked in and carried her things up before setting out to find the main office of Healthcare for All.

Ten minutes later, she smiled at the girl at the front desk and showed her work badge. "I'm Adrian Stewart with MidUSLogIn Inc., here to see Grayson Roberts."

The pictures on the walls drew her focus as the girl picked up her phone and called Gray. The decorations were typical of most companies like this one, photos of nurses with the patients, all smiling and happy. Were any of the people pictured actual clients or models they'd hired for the ads? So far, she hadn't seen the same ones at any of the other locations.

She turned as Gray walked through the door from the back of the building. He was more handsome in person than he'd been on her computer screen, and his smile came across even warmer, if that were possible. It was almost bright enough she didn't notice the bad fluorescent lighting.

It only took him three strides to reach her and enthusiastically pump her hand. "It's so nice to meet you in person."

She looked up, realizing he was much taller than she'd pictured him in her mind—and she was five-seven. "Nice to meet you too."

"Come on back, and we'll get started."

As he wound his way back through the hallways made by walls and partitions, she wondered if she'd ever remember how to get back out of this maze. This company had used every last inch of space in this building. Gray pointed out bathrooms and a breakroom and then took her down a flight of stairs to the basement. The air got cooler as they exited the stairwell.

"Welcome to the dungeon." He waved his hand around to encompass the hallway.

She lifted an eyebrow.

"IT jokes that they put us in the dungeon since we're down here in the basement. We keep it pretty cool down here because of the servers, so I hope you packed a jacket or sweater." He quickly walked to the end of the hallway and turned right, where his name was etched on the door's glass.

"This is my jail cell. Sorry about the mess. I started to straighten it up this morning since I knew you were coming, but then one of our servers went down and we had to deal with that. It never fails to happen on a day payroll has to be turned in."

"I know what you mean." She set her messenger bag on a chair just inside the door. "Do you guys have someplace for me to work while I'm here?"

"Hate to be the bearer of bad news, but you're sort of stuck with me. I'm clearing off that table, and we'll set your laptop up there." He pointed at a corner behind his desk, to a table crammed between a filing cabinet and the wall. "I know it's not fancy, but we'll make it work. All the offices are taken right now, so we're making do."

"I've had worse." She couldn't think of any off the top of her head, but she was raised to be polite. Picking up several old candy wrappers between two fingers, she dropped them in the wastebasket.

He gave her a sheepish grin. "I'm a slob. When you work in a dungeon, you tend to forget a lot of the etiquette things your parents tried to hammer into you growing up. Come with me, and I'll finish the tour and introduce you around."

There were three other IT guys down the hall. She'd memorize their names later. Today she just smiled and said *hello*. He showed her the conference room where their trainings would be next week. She nodded as she glanced at the setup.

"This is good. I'm guessing my computer screen will project on the wall?"

"There's a projector here." He pointed at the ceiling. "We have it aimed at the whiteboard so you can write on it if you need to. Fifteen laptops on each side for people to work and follow along. The training software is loaded and ready to go, and CJ will help make sure everyone's passwords work on

Tuesday morning. That gives us the rest of today, this weekend, and Monday to make sure everything else is ready."

"Let's get started then. I want to go over the program to confirm we have it set up like you guys wanted and check for quirks as we start using it. Then we need to go through a schedule for exactly what I'm teaching and make sure you understand everything, so you can help answer questions."

Ticking each item off on her fingers, she followed him back to his—their—office. "And I need to know exactly what our game plan is for the rollout and how we're going to make this work."

"You don't dawdle, do you?"

"No time. Your boss wants this done sooner rather than later. I take that seriously."

"I take it seriously, too, but I also don't plan to live here for the next month while it happens." He paused in the doorway. "Too much work and no play makes Gray a sad boy."

She shook her head. "I suppose you think you're taking off Monday for Memorial Day?"

"That would be nice."

"Don't hold your breath. As much as you've already done, I need a few more things completed before I'm ready for Tuesday. And the first thing we need to tackle is this table." She waved at the stacks of papers, random staplers, empty printer cartridges, and haphazard cables piled on what was to be her work area.

"Okay." He laughed. "Let's start with that." He grabbed all the cords, carried them down the hall.

She hummed as she stacked the papers neatly for him to sort through. Squinting a bit, she scanned the text. *I'm too young to start needing readers like Mom.* She glanced under the desk to see if she could add a lamp as well as her laptop.

"Drop something?"

She bumped her head on the table as she quickly straightened from her bent position. "Just looking to see if I could plug in a lamp. It's dark over here."

"I guess I never really noticed. It probably doesn't help that this light burned out." He pointed to the ceiling. "I'll put a ticket in."

She made quick work of the rest of the table and handed the piles to him when he turned around. "Chair?"

He hopped up to find her one.

Now the workspace was clear enough, she opened her laptop and waited for it to power up. The papers he'd dropped onto the corner of his desk slid off, landing on the floor behind her. She shook her head and knelt to pick them up again.

"Every time I come in here, you're on the floor." He pushed a chair in front of him.

Her cheeks heated. So much for making a good first impression. "Your papers slipped."

"That's what I get for being in a hurry." His grin eased her discomfort as he reached down to help her up. His hand was warm, despite the cold environment, and large enough to wrap around hers and graze her wrist.

Her fingers felt colder than before when he let go. She quickly turned to get everything going on her computer. Maybe focusing on something familiar would finally calm the butterflies that were even more fluttery since she'd first seen him walk into the foyer.

THE AIR in the small space they occupied filled with Gray's musky cologne, but not overwhelmingly. Instead, Adrian had to fight the urge to breathe it in more. His arm brushed against hers as he pointed to something on her computer screen. She shivered. Saturday had turned out rainy, too, and it made the basement of Healthcare for All even drearier ... and colder. At least, that's what she blamed for the chill.

"I warned you to bring a jacket." Gray got up to refill his coffee cup.

Adrian twisted around and pulled a cardigan out of her bag. "I have one. Just didn't want the bulkiness. Guess I'll have to give in anyway."

He brought the carafe and refilled her cup of coffee without her having to ask. "That should help a bit too."

"Thanks." She took a sip. "Are we about ready for next week?"

"Did you get that dropbox fixed?"

"See what you think." She turned her monitor his direction as he resumed his seat.

He leaned forward and took the mouse from her hand. She quickly pulled away, pretending she didn't feel a slight shock from the momentary contact. What was wrong with her? This was her coworker, nothing more.

"That's perfect." He sat back again and grinned at her. "Exactly what we were looking for."

"And we'll actually input all the client information as part of the training, right? So we don't need to load anything but our sample client?" She flipped through her notes.

"Right. And HR will work on employee information simultaneously, so we should have everything in place and everyone trained in time for the rollout on July first." He leaned back and crossed one leg over the other. "I think we're in a good place right now. Should be able to take Monday off after all, huh?"

"I guess things were more ready than I thought." She pushed the papers back into her bag. "The way Brad sounded on the phone earlier this week, I thought we'd be scrambling to get ready all weekend."

"With all the work we've done with your IT department and the emails you and I exchanged over the last few months, it's no wonder we're this ready. We've already gone through the schedule for training, so we'll jump in with one group next week. And another the week after."

"I'm amazed how organized you guys have all this." She

waved her hand around the conference room. "At some of the companies I've worked with over the last few years, I had to do everything when I got there. I feel like I'm not even earning my keep today."

He stood and stretched. "Don't worry. We'll get our money's worth out of you over the next few months."

She closed her laptop and wound up the cord. "Oh, I have no doubt. How well the training goes will determine how easily the rest of my time here goes, too. I know some people catch on faster than others."

"I'm sure you're a great teacher. Don't worry about it. I've been praying for things to go as smoothly as possible."

Adrian chose not to reply.

"Speaking of praying, since the rest of our weekend is free, would you like to join me for church tomorrow?" Gray threw his cup away and pushed in some chairs.

"No, thanks." Adrian forced a smile.

"Well, if you change your mind, you have my number. Give me a call. Bible class starts at nine." He walked out of the room with the carafe.

Adrian packed up the rest of her stuff and grabbed her keys. She'd forgotten how being in the Bible Belt was, with most people attending some sort of worship service on Sunday mornings. He came back in as she was leaving.

"Give me a second, and I'll walk you out."

She paused. He grabbed his things, turned off the lights, and strolled beside her down the hallway. It struck her how quiet and empty the building was. Now that they weren't focused on getting things ready for next week, she noticed Gray more than she had earlier too. Even his gait seemed happy. He pushed open the heavy front door of the building and opened an umbrella for them.

Their feet sloshed through the chilly puddles on the way to their cars. The umbrella was small enough that his arm touched hers. She tried to step a little farther away, despite the drips on her shoulder, but he followed her. The warmth of his body seeped through her sleeve. She quickly unlocked her door and climbed in the car, expecting him to turn and head to his own vehicle just as fast to get out of the rain.

"Don't forget my offer." He remained standing there, his umbrella over the opening so she wouldn't get as wet. "You'd be more than welcome to come to church with me."

"Thanks, but I don't do church. I'll see you bright and early Tuesday." She quickly pulled her door shut before he could comment on her statement. As she drove back to her hotel, she argued with herself. *That should help me get through this fixation I have for him. Maybe now I won't freak out every time his hand brushes mine or he smiles in my direction.* She turned into the parking lot and caught a whiff of his cologne from her sleeve. *Maybe not.*

SHE DIDN'T DO CHURCH. As if it were some kind of drug or something. Gray squirmed on the padded pew Sunday morning. Mom shot him a look, and he forced his legs to still.

Gray couldn't imagine a life without worshipping God. After all, God had saved him at fifteen—along with the help of his parents. His life wouldn't be anything as great as it was now without Him.

And he'd sworn he'd never even look twice at a girl who didn't love God more than himself. But here he was, having to admit the walls he thought so impermeable were crumbling after only a day and a half.

"Turn in your Bibles to Matthew chapter five, please."

Gray flipped through the pages of scriptures. He needed to focus on the sermon, not his new—temporary—coworker. He ran his finger down the lines until he came to the right verse.

"You are the light of the world." It was a passage he knew well. After all, he'd sung it with the kids at VBS many summers.

"Let your light shine before others, so that they may see your good works and give glory to your Father who is in heaven."

Is that why God had put Adrian in his life ... and his office? Was he supposed to be showing her God's love? Besides scaring her off with his mention of prayer and his invitation to worship services, had he done anything anyone else wouldn't have?

And if all he was supposed to do was reach out to her as a lost soul, why did his heart trip over itself at the sight of her every time he came around the corner? Why did he notice her light floral perfume or her long brown hair? Why did her humming show tunes under her breath as she worked make him so ridiculously happy?

God, I need your help. You know my history. You know my reasons. Please, God, if this isn't from you, take it out of my heart.

Mom nudged him as she stood to sing the invitation hymn. Somehow, he'd missed the rest of the lesson, lost in his thoughts. He quickly joined the rest of the congregation and went through the motions of singing and praying. But his heart remained focused much more on someone who wasn't there than on those who were.

"Where were you this morning?" Mom lifted an eyebrow at him after the final prayer.

"Right next to you. How did you miss it?" He winked.

"You know what I mean." She waggled a finger at him. "Your body was here, but your mind was somewhere else."

How much could he tell her? He was making so much out of something he didn't even understand. Would she think he was being ridiculous? Like he did.

"Grayson." Mom squeezed his hands. "Talk to me when you're ready."

"Gray." Dad appeared at his elbow after leading singing. "Naomi looks like she's lecturing you."

"Not lecturing. Just curious what has him so preoccupied." Mom flashed Dad a look Gray hadn't seen in a while—she wanted to fix what was wrong.

"Naomi, you know you can't always make things right. He's grown up now. He has to take care of the problems in his life." Dad raised both brows. "If he wants help, he knows he can ask us for anything."

Gray shook his head. "I'm fine, really. We're switching to a new program at work, and the consultant got thrown into my little office space, so things are cramped. But it's only temporary."

Only temporary, he reminded himself. Adrian wasn't going to be living here forever. No point in figuring anything out. *Guard your heart and wait for the Lord.*

Easier said than done.

"We'll be praying all goes well." Mom patted his arm.

"Thanks." He grinned. "How about lunch?"

"Now you sound like a teenager I used to know." Mom gave him an affectionate grin, clasped his arm, and followed him out of the building.

Nothing like time with God and his parents to help ground him once more. Here's hoping the attitude would hold when he faced temptation again on Tuesday.

5

A drian always had just a twinge of nervousness the first morning of training a new group. Something about talking in front of people set her belly to jumping. She sipped some coffee, then set it aside. She could drink more later, after her tummy was used to the thought of being still again.

A quick glance in the mirror showed her hair doing its normal wave in the opposite direction of where her curling iron had tried to coax it that morning. A rumble from the fifth day of rainy weather confirmed nothing would change it. She grabbed her keys and headed out.

Her weekend had flown by. She woke up Sunday morning earlier than normal, with enough time to get ready and attend worship services with Gray. She shook off the idea easily enough. Instead, Fred Astaire and Ginger Rogers had danced across her television screen while she snuggled up on the couch with a blanket and coffee. Monday had been much the same but with different actors.

She hummed a song from one of the movies she'd watched as she pulled into the parking lot. Smoothing down the front of her sweater, she climbed out of her car and dashed through the drizzle. As she stood under the overhang for a moment, catching her breath, she caught a glimpse of herself in the window and frowned—her hair looked even worse.

"Ugh!"

Normally, she wouldn't have minded much, but this morning was a bit like the first day of going to a new school all over again —she had to make a good impression. It was impossible to clear that thought from her head, try as she might. She'd only be here for a few months, so it shouldn't matter. But it did.

The girl at the front desk waved as Adrian walked through the entry and turned down the hallway. She wound her way back through the maze of offices and cubicles to the basement. The conference room was all set up, and the projector already shone on the whiteboard. Gray walked in right behind her with two carafes full of coffee.

"Good morning!"

He was way too chipper for a Tuesday after a holiday. She pulled her laptop out and set it up so there would be more than just a blank light on the marker board. Her background appeared, a picture from *Meet Me in St. Louis* with Judy Garland taking most of the foreground. She clicked into the application to get the program running and make sure all was in order before staff arrived.

Brad had touched base with her early this morning just to confirm everything was going smoothly. She assured him it was. Even though he was only a few years older than her, sometimes he seemed more like a father.

"Everything good to go?" Gray stared over her shoulder.

"Looks good to me. You said you wanted to talk first, right?" She tried not to breathe in his cologne too deeply. When he straightened, she shifted so there was a little more distance between them.

"Yeah. Just sort of wake everyone up and remind them of deadlines and stuff. We're all getting mandatory overtime right now to make sure all is in place and ready to go in three weeks. That gives us a week to work out any kinks. I'm not expecting any, but just in case. Maybe we won't have to stay too terribly late each day if I can get full cooperation from everyone."

A woman walked in, about five feet tall with a tight bun and glasses on a chain around her neck. "Are we ready?"

Gray motioned with his hand. "Adrian, this is Maggie Adams, head of our HR Department. She'll make sure we get all the employee information squared away upstairs while the office staff works on client information down here."

Adrian stepped forward and greeted the lady. "Great. Any questions for me? I know Brad and Michael have helped you get trained behind the scenes, but I'm available now if anything has come up since then."

"I think we're okay for now, but I'll be sure to come grab you if we run into anything today."

Adrian nodded and went back to her laptop while Gray and Maggie talked. Employees slowly filed in and took places around the room, most looking like Adrian felt—as if it were a Monday instead of a Tuesday. She put the screen to blank until time to start.

"GOOD MORNING!" Gray chuckled at the groans floating around the room. "Do we need to get up and dance around to get your blood flowing this morning?"

Boos followed that question.

"Come on! Okay, we have coffee and doughnuts in the back. Go get a cup and plate and see if the sugar and caffeine help, and then we'll get started for real." Gray stepped over to Adrian's side as people began to check out the food in the back. "Do you want anything?"

"Not yet. I might grab a bite during the break later, but I'm not much of a breakfast person."

"Not a church person, not a breakfast person—I wonder

what kind of a person you are." He cocked an eyebrow at her before walking back to the center of the room.

Was he flirting with her? Hadn't he promised to maintain distance? Hopefully, switching his focus to work mode would help.

"So, to get everyone relaxed and get our brains functioning a little more as the coffee kicks in, let's play some trivia. Our wonderful advertising department has hooked us up with some great prizes, so the more you play, the more likely you are to go home with something amazing."

Several people rolled their eyes. He knew what they probably expected—cheap ballpoint pens and can cozies. But he'd pulled a few strings.

"Okay, I've got some movie trivia, and the winner gets this cute little jar of candy." He held it up to show off all the chocolate bars inside.

Had Adrian just squirmed? When he glanced over, she wiggled the mouse on her computer and focused on her screen. Maybe he was seeing interest where there wasn't any. Just as well. If films made her as happy as they did him, he was in serious trouble.

He ran his finger down his list of facts, finding a good one. "The last line of this movie was also one of the last lines of the movie, *What's Up Doc?* Interestingly enough, both movies starred Ryan O'Neal."

Crickets. No one said anything. Gray scanned the room with an expectant glance. Adrian shifted in her seat. Did she know? No one spoke.

"*Love Story*." Adrian's voice came out somewhere between a whisper and a normal speaking level.

Gray pointed at her and grinned. "Exactly. Thank you, Adrian. How about this one? Name the British film which gave us a comedic spin on King Arthur and his Knights of the Round Table.'"

Adrian leaned back in her seat. Gray studied all the others in the room, including several men who ought to know such an easy answer. But again, no one uttered a sound.

"Really? No one knows?" Gray asked. He hadn't thought he'd chosen hard films.

"Is it *Goonies?*" A girl held her hand halfway up.

Gray shook his head. "No. Anyone else?"

A few more seconds passed before Adrian answered again. "*Monty Python.*"

"That's two for Adrian. She must be a movie buff!" *Lord, help me.* "Okay. One more. Can you tell me the motion picture featuring an archeologist who races Nazis to find a religious artifact?"

The *Jeopardy* theme song might as well have been playing. Sung by a symphony of crickets. This was getting ridiculous. Wasn't this movie another guy *must see?* Or was he just raised on older movies than other guys were?

"One more clue: the archeologist is afraid of snakes."

Finally, a guy in the back called out, "*Indiana Jones.*"

"Can you tell me which one?" Gray raised an eyebrow.

"That one was *Raiders of the Lost Ark*, right?"

"Right!" Gray gave a thumbs up. "Good job, Jeff! Okay, that's it for now. We'll do some more throughout the day and see who gets the most correct. So far, Adrian is in the lead. She's here with us for the next six weeks or so to help us learn how to use this great new software and transition to using it as our main system. Everyone, make her feel welcome."

"Oh, you're ready for me?" Adrian stood.

Should he have said something else? She probably wouldn't appreciate him spilling his knowledge of her tendency to hum. Or how attracted he was to her. Before he could figure out an answer, she'd walked to the front of the room to begin. Just as well, since they had a lot of ground to cover before the first scheduled break.

"I know you guys have already seen the introductory video, so today, we'll work in the program and let you try things out. A

41

training version has been installed on each of these laptops, so let's get you logged in so you can follow me as I show you step by step how to use this software."

Watching Adrian in her teaching groove was a thing of beauty. The way she phrased instructions, making sure everyone knew not only the correct terminology but also the words they'd probably use more often, like 'thingamajig,' made the lessons less boring and more down to earth. She moved quickly too. No dragging out instructions for this girl.

After an hour and a half, they called a short break. He shadowed Adrian as she filled a cup with coffee and took it to the kitchenette to reheat. She shut her eyes for a moment as the microwave worked its magic.

"Everything okay?" Gray hated to interrupt what appeared to be a much-needed moment of peace, but he had to make sure she didn't need anything else.

"Great. Just can't handle lukewarm coffee." She pulled the cup from the microwave and blew at the steam. "Everything going like you expected it to?"

"Faster, actually." He leaned against the counter. "You don't mess around when you train."

"Do you think I'm going too fast? To me, it's so easy to pick up, I just go through it and expect everyone to catch on as quickly as I did the first time. But sometimes I forget I helped develop this software, so it's second nature to me."

"Nah." He followed her back out to the hallway. "It sounds like everyone is understanding pretty well. I'm sure they'll ask more questions tomorrow when they're actually using the software and inputting client information."

"Yeah. Tomorrow night is probably going to be a late one."

"Not too late, I hope. Wednesday evenings I have Bible study."

She glanced over at him. "You said it was mandatory overtime. Doesn't that mean everyone has to stay until it's done? You might have to miss it for one week."

He pointed upstairs. "I've already okayed it with my boss. If all else fails, I can go to Bible study and then come back to work some more afterward. She knows God comes first for me."

"That's insane. Do you realize how late you might end up working if you do that?"

"It's worth it." He started back into the conference room.

And that discussion was a great reminder of what he'd sworn to himself several times now. Even if a woman met all his other requirements, including a love of movies and music—and long brown hair—he couldn't let those take precedence over her also having a relationship with God. No God in her life, no woman in his.

All he had to do now was remind his heart several times a day for the next six weeks.

———

SHE STARED after him for a moment. It had been a long time since she'd met anyone this crazy about religion. Had she ever met anyone this crazy? She shook her head and walked back into the conference room to prepare for the next part of their training. Gray stood up and started more movie trivia. She tried not to listen, but she couldn't help herself. Which film would he throw out now?

"Here's an easy one to get us started. This storyline has it all —a pirate, a swordsman, a giant, miracles, a pretty girl, and kissing."

She coughed to cover up her snort of amusement. It was a great description, and immediately told her what the movie was. Several other hands went up, and the first one correctly guessed *The Princess Bride*. She was glad not to come to Gray's rescue this time. She mentally nodded. That's what had prompted her to answer earlier—she felt bad no one had guessed his trivia.

"Okay. One more." Gray scrutinized everyone. Going back to

43

Great Brittain, this film is about a flower girl, a phonetics professor, and a colonel from India."

Adrian bit her tongue. Audrey Hepburn was one of her favorite actresses. She held her breath as a minute ticked by and no one answered.

Gray glanced her direction and she looked away. She would not save him again. This was getting absurd.

"How about a hint?" Gray tapped his finger against his chin. "The actress starts out with a thick cockney accent and ends with people thinking she's royalty."

Still no one replied. Several people peered her way. She pursed her lips.

Finally, she couldn't take it any longer. "*My Fair Lady*."

"Right again! We'll do another couple questions after lunch, but you guys will have a hard time beating Adrian. She's got three now." Gray's voice sounded proud of her. He stepped aside so she could take over again.

Squaring her shoulders, she stood to take them back to software training. That cup of coffee had her a bit jittery. She caught a glance of Gray shooting her a huge grin and refocused on her screen. What was going on? She wouldn't even be here long enough to really get to know him. *He's just a nice coworker. Quit letting him get under your skin.*

"Okay. Let's put in a pretend client and go through all the steps so you can see what you'll be doing tomorrow." She clicked on the box to enter the client's name and typed "Grayson" before she even knew she was doing it.

6

"Isn't there supposed to be a walking cane option on this dropdown menu?" A girl in the front row waved Adrian over the next afternoon as everyone worked to input client information. Adrian's training part was done for this week, and now she was here to make sure everything worked correctly and help answer questions as they practiced using the software.

She quickly inspected the menu and confirmed *walking cane* was indeed missing. "Let me see what I can do."

Adrian clicked through several pages on her laptop and added the missing item. She saved it and stood up. "Everyone, please stop for a moment and hit F5 on your keyboard. Let's refresh those screens and see if the menu updated."

It took a few moments, but the girl nodded confirmation. Adrian went back to walking around, making sure everyone did what they should. This was when she felt like a teacher, ironic since education was Danielle's major, not hers. Gray stuck his head in the doorway and motioned to her.

"What's up?" She followed him out to the hallway.

"How are things going?"

She rubbed the back of her neck. "Fairly well. Not quite as

quickly as I'd hoped, probably about a fifth of the way through this section of clients."

They'd divided the clients between this training group and the other group that would train next week. The ones not in training were holding down the office and making sure the regular day-to-day things got done.

"Do you think we'll be about halfway through by five?" He leaned against the wall.

She shook her head. "Probably not. Some of them keep asking the same questions over and over again, so that's delaying the input."

"How late do you think we should have them stay tonight since we're doing this again tomorrow?"

Pursing her lips, she tapped a finger on her chin. "We're also going over some payroll stuff tomorrow, so we won't have the whole day to finish this up. I'd say let's see where we are at five and go from there."

He glanced at his watch. "It's four now. Give me a minute and I'll come in and help you guys knock a few out. We had a problem with the phones at one of our other offices, so I've been playing phone tag with the provider to try and get that straightened out all afternoon. I just need to double-check one more thing, and I should have that problem fixed."

"Sounds good."

Several minutes later, he came in and wrote *198* on the whiteboard. "This is how many we've entered so far. We need to be a lot closer to five hundred before we leave here tonight. I'm helping, so let's have a contest. Make a pile of the ones you've done from this point out, and whoever has the most wins one of our prizes."

Great idea.

He sat down next to her and logged in. "Okay, give me a few clients to enter. Let's see who can do it the fastest."

"You're on." After slapping a stack in his hand, she picked up some for herself to work on too. "Even with me getting interrupted to answer questions, I'll probably still beat you."

"We'll see about that."

Someone brought a speaker and hooked their phone up so they could listen to music. The sounds of clicking and typing filled in the few spaces where the radio was silent. An hour sped by as Adrian entered client after client, piling up her stack of *done*. She had to get up to answer questions only four times.

Gray glanced at his watch, stood up, and stretched. "Okay. Five o'clock. Everyone finish the one you're working on right now and count up how many you've completed so we can see where we're at." He went around and added up everyone's numbers.

Having done fifteen, Adrian figured no one had beaten her, but she still waited to see.

On the whiteboard, Gray added two-hundred twenty-five to the one-hundred ninety-eight that had already been up there. "We're at four-hundred twenty-three right now, and it's almost five. We need several people to stay and knock out some more to get us to five hundred before we quit tonight."

"Who won the contest?" Jeff called from the back of the room.

Gray glanced at Adrian, and she cocked an eyebrow at him. He grinned and looked back out at the rest of the room. "I did."

"What?" The exclamation slipped from Adrian before she could help herself.

"I did sixteen, one more than you."

"Adrian, it's not letting me put this address in." A girl in the back waved a paper at her.

Reluctantly, Adrian got up and went to help the girl instead of staying to recount Gray's stack of clients he'd input. Several people left since they'd achieved so much of their goal by five. The rest of them knocked out the remaining work. They finished by five-thirty, shut down laptops, and filed out.

With the music turned off, quiet settled over the area. Adrian checked her email to make sure she hadn't missed anything important in the last few hours. She wasn't paying much attention to anything around her. Her brain was already on everything she needed to go over with them tomorrow.

"Did you know you hum?"

She started as Gray's voice tickled her ear.

He grinned at her sheepishly. "I wasn't trying to make you jump."

"I didn't realize everyone else was gone." She closed her laptop and wrapped up her power cord.

"People tend to get out of here pretty quickly at the end of the day."

"I guess I can understand that." She loaded her messenger bag and looked around for anything she might need tonight when she reviewed completions and what still needed done.

"You didn't answer my question." Gray leaned lazily against the table, his legs in front of him blocking her exit.

"Question?"

"Did you know you hum?"

Did she have to admit it? It had been a bad habit her whole life. "Yes."

"Just making sure." He stood up. "I think it's cute."

Her heart sped up a bit, and she had to remind her legs to move so she could follow him out the door. What was this? High school?

"Don't you have a Bible study to get to?" She decided a change of subject was the only thing that might save this conversation from any further flirty comments. Especially a subject that would remind her again why he was completely off-limits to her. She had no interest in getting involved with a Christian.

"Yes. I do. I was going to go grab a bite of dinner and head straight there. Would you like to join me?"

She'd opened herself up for that one. "No, thanks. Remember?"

"Yes. I know. You said you're not a church person or a breakfast person. You're obviously a movie person and a humming person. See? I'm figuring you out."

She veered off and headed to her car, hoping she could distance herself from his observations. She wasn't sure she wanted him to figure her out. What good could come from it?

"Have a good night, Adrian." Gray waved from his vehicle.

"You, too, Gray." She shut the door and drove away, even though her heart wanted to stay and see what else he might have noticed.

Later that evening, snuggled on the couch with her laptop, Adrian couldn't focus on what she needed to. She skimmed through the clients that had been entered, trying to watch for things that might be out of place. Instead, her mind wandered to what Gray had said about figuring her out.

Did she want to be analyzed? Usually she kept a wall up, not wanting anyone to get in. She'd started building it in high school. After moving four times between kindergarten and sixth grade, she'd grown tired of making friends only to have to leave them again. Instead, she embraced the 'new girl' aura. Most kids steered clear of new students until they saw if they fit in. Adrian made sure they didn't find out, or at least tried to.

Her family had stayed in one town in Middle Tennessee from sixth grade through eleventh, the longest they'd lived anywhere. She'd begun to let her fortifications down some, joined a few clubs in high school, and relaxed just a bit. It was a mistake. They moved again the summer before her senior year. Her high school ring remained unworn in a drawer of her jewelry box because it wasn't actually from the school where she graduated.

When she left for college, she knew it would be for only four years, so she'd built her barricades a little higher. Only a few people reached past them, one of them her roommate, with whom she still kept in contact. And then she'd taken a job where she knew she wouldn't be anywhere for long. That helped her reinforce her defenses yet again.

Even her family didn't truly get past her walls anymore. Granted, they had a whole different set of hurdles to leap besides the ones she used with everyone else. If only her dad hadn't raised her to believe God was loving and wanted the best for her. Maybe then it wouldn't have hurt so much when there were no real answers about why God would allow her to be ripped from her home again and again. Maybe it would be easier to be around her family as well.

That was the God Gray believed in too. Didn't he know that his God was a jerk? She shook her head. Gray needed to be off-limits as anything but a coworker. And she needed to stop thinking about her past and focus on all these clients before tomorrow morning.

7

"How are we looking?" Gray leaned back in his chair and glanced over his shoulder at Adrian as she worked at her space behind him. It was the end of the second training week, and everyone else had gone home except for a few HR people upstairs who were scurrying to get the rest of their part finished.

She clicked a few more things and hit *save*. "Not too bad. I think things will go a lot better if we plan to work at least part of tomorrow. We only have a couple more weeks left to make sure everything is functioning. We'll have to be running scenarios and testing things all next week to try and find as many issues as we can. That will let us work out kinks before we go live in July."

He nodded and crossed one leg over the other. "I can come in for a while tomorrow morning. Busy tomorrow afternoon."

"You're a veritable social butterfly." She glanced over her shoulder at him.

"I don't know about that, but I do stay fairly busy. Every time something comes up at church that needs volunteers, I try to sign up. Keeps me out of trouble."

She turned back to her computer. "If you say so."

He scooted her way. "And I enjoy it. It's nice to be able to focus time and energy on other people, be able to give back."

"'Do unto others.'" She held her fingers up to make air quotes. "Do you sign up to take meals to sick people? Or sew dresses for the widows?"

"I would love to take meals to people, but the women seem to think that's something only they can do. And I'm not exactly handy with a needle and thread." He wiggled his fingers at her. "These sausages can rebuild a hard drive but are useless when it comes to sewing on a button. You seem to know quite a bit about things Christians are supposed to be doing to serve others."

She chewed on her bottom lip. "It's pretty general knowledge."

Pretty general knowledge? About sewing dresses for widows? Only if you studied the Bible at some point in your life would you know about Tabitha doing that. There was more to Adrian Stewart than she was letting on. What had driven her to avoid God at all possible costs?

"Does this look right to you?" She pointed to her computer screen.

He leaned over her shoulder to get a better view. Did she sniff a little, like she appreciated the cologne he wore? Not that he could blame her. He felt the same way about her perfume. Just wasn't expecting the reciprocation.

His arm brushed hers as he pointed to the monitor. "This still needs to have a space for another phone number."

"Right."

Sitting back in his chair again, he put a few extra inches between them. It was getting too tempting to accidentally-on-purpose let his arm or hand bump into hers as they worked so closely. A few more clicks and the missing box was added. She saved her work and straightened the stacks of papers around her area. They were opposites in their cleanliness.

"You gone?" He looked up from his computer as she stood and stretched.

"Yeah. It's almost seven, and we'll be back again in the

morning. I figure I'll go grab a bite and take it back to my hotel, munch while I check emails, and see what all Brad thinks I'm not doing today."

He shook his head. "Everything he's ever said about you has been praises. I can't imagine him finding things you're doing wrong."

"It's probably not that bad. Has just felt like it the last few days as we try to get things hammered out and ready for testing next week. Seems like something has gone wrong at the end of every day this week." She slipped her messenger bag over her shoulder.

He held a finger up. "Nothing has gone wrong today."

"Thanks for jinxing my evening." She smiled. "See you around eight tomorrow morning?"

"Sounds great."

Adrian was a conundrum he pondered long after she was gone. Two weeks into this situation and he fought harder than ever not to think of her as possible girlfriend material. *She'll only be here another month or so, Gray. And she doesn't love God.*

Was there anything he could do about that? Either problem? Both?

"WHAT ARE YOU HUMMING?" Gray asked from behind her the next morning.

Adrian frowned for a moment. What had she been humming? "I don't even know now. I just hum whatever's in my head at the moment. It used to get me in trouble in school. I don't even realize I'm doing it. It drove the kids who sat around me crazy. Is it annoying you?"

"No. Just sounded familiar, but I couldn't place it."

With a nod, she went back to work.

A little later, he turned all the way around to face her. "That's one of our songs."

Confusion wrinkled her forehead. "What?"

"You're humming one of the songs we're singing tonight at the Golden Oldies banquet."

"What was I humming?"

"'Singin' in the Rain,' right?" He motioned as if he were holding an umbrella.

She thought for a moment before nodding. "That's probably what it was. I watched it the other day and the songs stuck in my head ever since."

"What part do you sing?"

"Alto." She answered before thinking.

"Ha!" He pointed at her. "I knew you were a church girl at heart."

"What?" What had she said?

"Only people who go to church or have been in a choral group usually know what part they sing. You don't strike me as the kind of girl who was in a chorus, so I'm betting you used to go to church."

She turned back to her computer. Maybe if she ignored him, he'd take the hint and drop the subject.

"I'm right, aren't I?" His voice was less gloating and more concerned now.

Most of her didn't want to talk about any of this, but she knew he wouldn't let it go if she didn't tell him something. "Yes. I used to go to church. Are you happy?"

"No."

She faced him once more. "What? I just admitted you were right. Why doesn't that make you happy?"

"Because it means something has come between you and God. And that doesn't make me happy." He leaned forward with his elbows on his knees. In this confined space, it put his face uncomfortably close to hers. His sunshiny grin wasn't in its usual place, and the wrinkles between his brows overshadowed the laugh lines by his eyes.

A lump filled her throat that took three swallows to move.

"Don't worry about me. I'm fine."

He took both her hands in his. "Are you really?"

She pulled away and stood up. "I said I'm fine. Taking a break, refill my coffee. I'll be back in a few minutes."

What was going on? One minute, they'd been working amiably together, and the next, the tension in the room had been so thick she needed a serrated knife to cut it. She took a long swig of coffee in the kitchenette down the hall from his office. How had they gone so quickly from a conversation about a song to him wondering about her relationship with God?

She dawdled back toward their office, stopping in the bathroom to splash some water on her face. Maybe all these late nights were catching up with her, and she was reading too much into everything he said. Next time, she wouldn't let Brad cut her vacation time short—she obviously needed more time off.

"Okay. I've got three things I need your help on." He looked up as she walked back through the door.

She quietly released a breath she'd been holding and straightened her shoulders. They were back to work. This she could handle. She pulled her chair up beside him and helped him walk through the problems he'd discovered.

The rest of the morning was fairly uneventful. She tried not to hum as she worked alongside him to fix a few things before lunch. While they wrapped up one last issue, his cell phone rang.

As he answered, she gathered her things. They were at a point where they wouldn't have to stay any longer today. She placed her laptop into her bag as he hung up.

"Got any plans for tonight?" He wore a look somewhere between innocence and mischief.

"Just work."

He shook his head. "We're far enough along you don't need to work again until Monday."

"I just want to go over a few things." She slipped the strap over her shoulder. "Brad says I'm a perfectionist."

"Possibly. But that doesn't mean you need to go over

anything tonight. You've been working too hard. You're looking worn down."

"Aww, thanks." She patted the bags under her eyes. She didn't need the reminder they were there. "If you're going to talk to me like that, I'm definitely just going back to my hotel. This," she pointed to her messenger bag, "is way more inviting than being told I look exhausted."

"That," he pointed as well, "can wait. I need a favor."

The intrigue drew her in against her will. What was he about to ask her to do? "Um..."

"One of our entertainers for the banquet tonight just caught strep throat and can't come. We need an alto." He gave her a sheepish look.

"Sorry. No way." She held her hands up and backed towards the door. "No."

"Adrian, come on. I just have this feeling they're songs you know—"

"Gray, just because I know a song doesn't mean I want to sing it."

"They're not hymns." His hands reached out in supplication as he stood. "The most church-y thing that might happen is a prayer before the meal."

She hated herself immediately, but she stopped to listen. "I can't. I can't go back in a church building. It's a long story, and I know you don't understand, but I can't do it. I promised myself."

He paused a moment, and she hoped he'd give up.

"It's in the fellowship hall."

No such luck.

"Which is actually across the parking lot from the main church building. This isn't a worship service. It's a dinner my friends and I are putting on for the older members. We're singing old songs from the forties and fifties and around then. That's all. You'd get a free meal." He gave her what she could only call a puppy dog look.

"Gray—"

"Please?"

"You don't even know if I can sing. All you've ever heard me do is hum." She grasped at any straw she could come up with. And she was running out quickly.

"Call it instinct."

"I have nothing to wear." That was her last excuse. How had he breached so many of her barriers?

"I know just the thing. Let's go drop off your car at your hotel, grab lunch—my treat—and let me introduce you to a great friend of mine, Lucy. She runs a thrift store."

Adrian felt slightly dizzy. Was she actually going to do this? She, who didn't ever put herself out there in a social situation? Could she just slip through the sidewalk now, please? If that were a prayer, God didn't answer it, either.

8

Adrian readily admitted she missed southern barbeque. She'd tried quite a few versions as she worked different places the last few years, but nothing compared to Tennessee, and especially Memphis. Gray treated her to a pulled pork sandwich that had her sighing with contentment.

"Good?" He grinned at her from across the table.

"So good. I always forget how great this tastes until I'm back in an area that has it." She licked some sauce off her fingers.

"I don't think I could stand to live somewhere that didn't have pulled pork."

She shrugged. "You get used to it, eat ribs and other things. It's not the same, but it'll do in a pinch."

"Are you originally from St. Louis?" He popped a French fry in his mouth.

"No. Just always wanted to live there."

"Cardinals fan?"

A laugh burst from her. "No. Not really. I'm not sure what made me pick St. Louis. I don't have any family there. No history. It just always called to me. When Brad and Michael were hiring for my position, it seemed serendipitous."

He pointed a fry at her. "Some people would call it a God-thing."

"Some would. God doesn't work that way in my life." She took another bite, not wanting to continue this train of conversation. Why did it always come back to this with Gray? She'd enjoyed their lunch until now.

"You said it was a long story. Want to share?" He took a sip of sweet tea and leaned back in his chair.

"Not really. I'd rather think about other things right now." She finished her last fry and took a drink. "What exactly are you wanting me to sing tonight?"

A look crossed his face, saying he might protest her change of topic. But then he leaned forward with his elbows on the table. "You already know about 'Singin' in the Rain.'"

She nodded.

"We're also doing 'As Time Goes By,' 'Unchained Melody,' 'Swinging on a Star,' and a medley of songs about traveling that include 'Come Fly with Me,' 'Chattanooga Choo Choo,' 'Surrey with the Fringe on Top,' and 'The Trolley Song.'" He tapped a straw against the table as he listed each song. "Any of those you don't know?"

She shook her head. "I know them well enough to sing along if I have the lyrics in front of me." She could sing "The Trolley Song" in her sleep, but she wasn't going to mention that.

"I thought you might." Leaning back, he grinned.

"Why?"

"Why, what?"

She pointed at herself. "Why did you think I'd know those songs? A lot of people wouldn't. They're from the forties and fifties, not our generation."

"I've heard you humming and picked out at least two of them." He held his hand out and ticked off points. "I've also heard some of what you stream while you work. You were the only one able to name the older movies in my trivia last week. There's just something in you that strikes me as an 'old soul' who would like songs like that."

"I guess I was raised that way. Growing up, we watched a lot of old movies. My mom said we didn't have to worry as much about language or other things she didn't want us seeing. And I found more friends in the older ladies at church than in kids my age. I guess it rubbed off." She fiddled with a napkin, then glanced up to find him studying her. What was he figuring out now?

"That's not necessarily a bad thing. It has definitely come in handy today."

"For you, anyway. I'm still not too sure about any of this."

He glanced at his watch and then jumped up, pulling her with him. "We've got to go if we're going to find you something to wear. The girls are trying to dress at least semi-vintage and have been raiding their grandmas' closets and thrift stores for weeks. We've only got this afternoon. Come on!"

THAT EVENING, Adrian faced the fellowship hall where Gray attended church. She swallowed a lump in her throat and smoothed out the blue skirt of the dress she'd found in Gray's friend's thrift store that afternoon.

It wasn't a completely accurate replica of a forties dress, but it was close enough she decided it would work. The boat neck accented her shoulders, and the safety pins pulled in the sides where it was slightly too big, only making the circle skirt seem even fuller. She'd convinced Gray to let her go back to her hotel to change and get ready before meeting him here.

But as she stood in the parking lot, she had more doubts than ever about being here. They could do without one alto. He'd said there were about ten people who were supposed to sing. One wouldn't be missed that much. She reached for her car door to flee the scene when Gray came running out of the building.

"There you are!"

She bent over to pretend like she was picking up something she'd dropped. Maybe he wouldn't notice how close she'd been to driving away. She squared her shoulders as she stood back up. "Here I am."

He was dapper in his navy suit and a tie the exact color of his blue eyes.

"You look great. Very retro." His blue eyes sparkled as he took in her outfit. "Even your hair looks legit. The girls have been bemoaning the fact they couldn't get their hair to do whatever it is they wanted it to do." He gestured at his own waves as if he had no idea what he was talking about, then offered his arm. "Shall we?"

She tried to control the trembling of her hand as she tucked it in his elbow and let him lead her into the building. She hadn't been in a church facility in four years. And the last few times she'd let her parents coerce her into going, she wasn't comfortable. *It's just a dinner. God won't strike you dead for being here.*

Swing music played softly in the background. People milled around, chatting with each other, pointing out different aspects of the decorations, laughing as if nothing were amiss. And nothing was, except her. White tablecloths adorned tables with pretty glass candle holders in the middle. Black-and-white pictures of former movie stars were stapled to the walls.

If she weren't so nervous, she'd have loved this. Gray led her through the crowd, greeting several people as he walked past them to the kitchen.

"Ta-da!" He presented her to the people in the kitchen with a flourish. "This is my friend, Adrian. She's an alto."

Friend? When did we go from coworker to friend? She quickly shook the thought from her head and tried to pay attention as he introduced her to everyone else. She wouldn't remember most of their names, but maybe she could catch one or two.

"Your hair looks amazing." A girl he called Christine or Christa or Cassie, or something like that, came over to look at Adrian's coiffure.

Adrian reached back to make sure all her bobby pins were still in place. "It's not much. I watched a couple videos online, pulled out my hot rollers and pins, and figured it out close enough."

A girl Gray had introduced as Victoria joined them. "We should get together soon so you can help us learn too. I'm not good at watching videos to figure things out, but maybe if someone shows me—"

"I won't exactly have a lot of free time while I'm here." Adrian took a step back. She hated being the center of attention.

"Are we ready to get started? I have a feeling our guests are going to be hungry soon, and it is past time to begin." Gray came to her rescue.

They all filed out, and Gray whistled to gain everyone's attention. The honorees took their seats, laughing and obviously already having a good time. A hush fell over the room, and before Adrian could brace herself, one of the other guys led them in a prayer. She ducked her head automatically but didn't close her eyes. As the thanks for the food wrapped up, she lifted her head and saw Gray watching her. He winked.

Victoria and Christine—*that* was her name!—grabbed her to help deliver salads to tables.

"I'm Gray's coworker." She gave general answers as people asked questions. "Just in town for a little while. Yes, it's a lovely dinner." After a little while, the awkwardness fell away, and she relaxed.

As Gray came out of the kitchen with a tray full of spaghetti, she bumped into him and reached out to steady things before they crashed. His fingers brushed hers as he shifted his grip, and a shiver ran through her arms. Had he felt it too?

"You look like you're having fun. Want to help me exchange salad plates for these?" He nodded at the food in his arms.

Evidently, he hadn't noticed the weird static electricity or whatever it was that seemed to keep happening between them. "Sure."

Each person got Gray's undivided attention as he served them. He had to be one of the most selfless people she'd ever met. *What must his childhood have been like for him to turn out so nicely? Probably perfect.* She shook away that bitter thought and smiled when a lady complimented her outfit.

Before she was ready, they had served everyone dessert, and it was time to perform. Gray dragged her up to the front and placed her between Christine and Victoria. He slipped her the lyrics and then took his place with the other males. A guy named Nathan blew a pitch pipe, hummed a note, and then started to sing "Swinging on a Star."

Most of the words she knew by heart and only required a glance at the lyrics sparingly. At the beginning, she sang quietly, not wanting to draw any undue attention to herself. As the songs continued, though, her love of singing pulled her in, and she gave herself over to the music, a smile lighting her face. She'd forgotten how great *a capella* music sounded.

Singing about ducks and chicks scurrying away from the surrey, she caught Gray's glance and grinned at him. Yes. She was glad he'd dragged her into this.

"Your voice is so great." Victoria touched her shoulder when they were done. "Did you sing in a chorus or something growing up?"

Adrian shook her head. "I just love to sing."

"I only wish my alto were that nice. I always seem to look at the wrong note and get confused as to which part I'm actually singing. I think sometimes the sopranos wish I would just go down and sing bass instead of jumping up and joining their part." Christine pointed to the notes on Adrian's music.

"I didn't notice anything wrong when you sang." Adrian gave her a smile.

While the others gathered the dessert plates still scattered around the room, Adrian offered to work on dishes so they could continue to chat with the guests. She slipped her heels off and wrapped an apron around her waist to protect at least part of her dress. The soapy water was comforting, and she quickly found a rhythm as she scrubbed, rinsed, and dried pots and pans.

Gray stuck his head back through the kitchen door. "We're about to wrap things up if you'd like to join us." He held out his hand to her.

She wiped the soapy water off her own and then reached out to accept his grasp. He didn't let go as they walked back out into the main part of the fellowship hall. They joined in the circle forming as everyone in the room clasped hands and spread out to make sure no one was left out.

"We want to thank everyone for coming this evening. We hope you all enjoyed it as much as we did. As we wrap up this evening together, we'll end the way we always finish events here at East Poplar. Let's sing."

Voices all over the room joined in. The words came automatically to Adrian's mouth, lyrics she had sung growing up. She wouldn't give in and let them out, though.

The song was short, but full of words she no longer believed. Her experience hadn't had people with a common love. The strength, hope, and joy mentioned near the end—they didn't exist in her memory of God's people.

The last words reverberated off the walls. Adrian stared at the floor as Gray led everyone in a closing prayer. She wiggled her still-bare toes and tried to fight whatever was bubbling inside of her. These people really seemed to live the words of the song, better than probably any church her family worked with while she was growing up. But that didn't mean they weren't just as mean and hurtful as people had been to her family time and time again through the years.

She quickly let go of the hands on either side of her as Gray said, "Amen." There weren't many dishes left. She would help with a few more and then head back to her hotel—where she should have stayed in the first place this evening.

"Cute toes." Gray's voice sent a shiver down the back of her neck as he whispered in her ear while dropping a few more pieces of silverware in the water.

She splashed in his direction. He just grinned and went back out to help move tables around. The other girls chattered around her, but she wasn't listening. She set the last few things on the drying pad and slipped her shoes back on. Maybe she could sneak out and avoid anyone inviting her to join them for church in the morning.

WHERE WAS SHE? He didn't see that gorgeous blue dress—or the beautiful woman it belonged to—anywhere. If he were a betting man, he'd lay money she was leaving without saying goodbye.

Just like she'd wanted to when he caught her in the parking lot at the beginning. Oh, she wouldn't admit it, but he'd seen the signs in her eyes and posture. He'd worn that look himself too many times not to recognize it in others.

He opened the glass doors and glanced across the parking lot. There. She must be only a moment ahead of him because she hadn't gone far. Either that or those shoes were hurting worse than he thought.

"You trying to sneak off?" Gray ran up beside her as she walked to her car.

"I was." She took a deep breath of the night air. "Should've known you wouldn't let me."

"I would like the chance to say thanks again for coming tonight. I thought you enjoyed it." He leaned against her car door so she couldn't open it without being completely rude.

She just nodded. He hummed "As Time Goes By" under his breath, the last song they'd sung before "A Common Love." The words ran through his head, mocking all his attempts over the last few weeks to put her out of his mind. Lyrics about a kiss —dangerous.

The vehicle gave a sharp beep, jerking him from his

stargazing. She lifted her thumb from the unlock button on her key fob. Lazily, so as not to show how his heart raced, he stood up straight.

Much as he'd like to continue in the line of thought the song had started, her stance told him *not a chance*. But he'd be remiss if he didn't once more offer his standing invitation. The one he'd offered every Sunday and Wednesday she'd been here.

"I don't suppose ..."

"No." She shook her head adamantly. "I'll see you Monday, Gray."

"Bright and early." He reached out and squeezed her arm. "Don't work too hard tomorrow."

IF GRAY THOUGHT Adrian had tugged at his heartstrings when he first glimpsed her on the video chat and then pulled harder when she hummed and answered movie trivia, listening to her sing had just about done him in.

Working side by side as they were most days, he'd learned to read her moods—the giveaway was the song in her head. She tapped her pencil against the desk when trying to figure something out. And all her catchphrases he knew by heart.

You've got to be kidding me was at the top of the list.

Two weeks into her stint with their company and the training was done. The software would go live in a few more weeks, and they'd run their first payroll out of it. Adrian scrambled to help enter the rest of the data, fix problems that appeared during testing, and answer questions both in Memphis and St. Louis. He'd loved her training mode, but her everyday work mode was hardcore. She was like one of those bunnies with the battery in back—she didn't stop.

Diane stuck her head in the doorway. "Gray, we're having that same problem again."

He held up a finger, hit *save*, and scooted around Adrian to get out. "Tell me which problem again. I've handled so many in the last few weeks I can't keep them all straight."

"The one we always have when we try to pull the reports for payroll." Diane huffed as they walked toward her office. "Remember when you had to come in and click something to get more numbers to show up on the spreadsheet? Before Adrian got here?"

"Let's look." He leaned over her computer and sighed. "Okay. I think I remember what I did. Give me a minute."

Diane flopped in a chair across from her desk and crossed her arms over her chest. "Are we going to still have these issues after moving to the MidUSLogIn software?"

"Not supposed to." Gray clicked several boxes and hit the button to rerun the report.

"What happens if we do?"

"Then we work with it and call Adrian and have her work with it. And we'll figure it out as we go. We've got a few more weeks to do test runs and make sure as many gremlins are out of the system as possible." He waved at the screen. "See if this looks better."

They switched places, and Diane nodded. "Better. Thanks."

"Diane, don't fret about the new program until we actually know what's going to happen. Adrian is working her tail off to make sure it all goes as smoothly as it can." Gray paused at the door to make sure she didn't need anything else.

"I wish we could keep her around. You're sometimes so busy working on other technical problems with phones and the servers and stuff, I can't always find you right away for this. Having someone on staff just for the software we use for most of our business would be beyond helpful."

"Agreed. But who knows what the budget could allow? Seems like the last time we asked for a staff member in that role, it wasn't an option." Gray tilted his head side to side. "Riley might say something different now, but I doubt it."

"Might be worth checking into anyway." Diane raised a brow.

"Maybe. But Adrian already has a job. What could possibly lure her into moving down here to Memphis and staying in one place for more than a few months? I bet our pay wouldn't be equal to what she gets now either."

"What could lure her down here, indeed?" Diane pursed her lips and shot him a look he wasn't sure he wanted to interpret.

"You good here?" He pointed to her computer.

"Until we have to close. I may need you again then."

"Just let me know." He tapped the doorframe and walked back down to his office.

Adrian's floral scent permeated the small space, and he fought the smile that jumped to his lips as he settled back into his seat. He was getting too used to having her next to him. If they did hire her, assuming she'd even want the position—the position that wasn't even real—she'd probably get her own office space. But it would still be closer than St. Louis.

And give him more time to try and figure out why she kept pushing God away from her life. And maybe other things?

"You fix the problem?" Adrian threw the question over her shoulder without looking away from her report.

"For now. Diane is worried about having similar problems with the MidUSLogIn software. I guess she's had to deal with these issues so long, she can't imagine something working better."

"I'm doing my best to make sure she doesn't have to deal with them anymore."

"And we appreciate it." Gray chuckled. "So much so that Diane even suggested we just keep you here forever."

"Much as I like Diane, I live in St. Louis." Adrian's voice was tight.

"I know." He couldn't say more. Her response had been the expected answer, but it still hurt. Why was she afraid of putting down roots? How could he get her to open up and tell him why she kept everything and everyone at arm's length?

69

9

"Look at this." Gray interrupted Adrian as she ran a scenario in their practice software the next Wednesday afternoon.

As she spun her chair around, she bumped into him with her legs. "Sorry. What's up?"

He pointed to his screen. "When we try to export the payroll, it isn't pulling everyone. This says we have only thirty employees. It should say over five hundred."

Scooting her chair closer, she reached for his mouse. "May I?"

He nodded permission and leaned back a little. She clicked through several things, looking for a box that hadn't been checked that might cause such a problem. About halfway through her scan, her cell phone rang behind her. He reached back and handed it to her.

"Hello?" She hadn't even checked the caller ID to see who was calling.

"Adie, guess who's going to be in Memphis this weekend." The sound of Danielle's voice made her smile.

"Please tell me not Mom and Dad."

"I have no idea what Mom and Dad are doing this weekend,"

Danielle said. "But my family will be there. Can we meet up somewhere? The boys would love to see you."

"Um ..."

"Oh, come on. You can get away for a few hours to see your nephews and your favorite sister."

"Danny, it's not that I don't want to see you. It's that we keep hitting snags with this software and only have about a week left to get everything running correctly so we can go live." Adrian sent a look of apology to Gray, but he just shrugged.

"Just a couple hours. Phil has a thing he needs to do for work there, so I figured the boys and I could tag along and eat lunch with you or something. You've got to eat, right?"

"Yes, I will probably eat sometime on Saturday." Adrian got up and stepped out in the hallway. "But I wasn't planning to leave the office to do it."

"You should go." Gray walked by her on his way down the hall.

"Who was that?" Danielle asked.

"Coworker. Head of the IT department here."

"There ya go. He's okay with you coming to eat lunch with us. I'm telling the boys you're coming, and then if you don't, you'll break their hearts. That way, I know you won't wiggle out of it."

If only she could stick her tongue out at her sister. But it would just elicit funny looks from anyone walking by.

"Fine. But not for long, okay? Just lunch."

"But the boys wanted to go to Bass Pro. You know that one in the Pyramid—it's huge."

"Danny! That's not anywhere near where I'm working right now." Adrian walked to the end of the hallway and into the stairwell to try to keep her conversation more private.

"At least think about it, okay? The boys hardly ever get to see you. We've got to take advantage of you being this close."

Adrian sighed. "I know. I want to spend more time with them too. It's just hard when I'm in the middle of a stint."

"I'll text you Friday to work out details, okay?" Danielle's voice sounded a lot like their mom's. It even had some of the same hints of hope and longing. Adrian couldn't remember hearing those there in the past.

"Okay. We'll text Friday."

"Love you."

"Love you too." Adrian hung up and pocketed her phone. She thought about banging her head against the concrete wall for a minute before leaving the stairwell, but that would only add to the headache she already had.

Gray looked up as she reentered their office. "Lunch date?"

Adrian nodded. "Saturday. I'll try not to take too long."

"Adrian, it's okay. You need to take more breaks. I keep telling you that. We can't have you completely burnt out before we go live. We'll need you even more then. Take the whole afternoon off Saturday."

"I did that last Saturday." She pointed to him. "You're not getting what you're paying for."

"I think I am. Go. Have fun with this Danny guy."

What did she hear in his voice? It couldn't be jealousy. She lowered herself into her chair. "Danny's my sister."

Gray's eyes were questioning. "Your sister's name is Danny?"

"Short for Danielle. She and her boys are coming up Saturday for her husband's work, and she wanted me to meet them at Bass Pro."

"The one in the Pyramid?"

She nodded and leaned forward to grab the mouse again. "Yep."

"I've been meaning to go see it ever since it opened, but I never seem to make it that far. I bet that would be fun." He sounded wistful.

"It's a guy thing, huh? A bunch of fish and guns and camo?" She grinned at him.

"Are you kidding? There's a huge aquarium, a marshy area with alligators, an arcade where you can practice shooting, a glass elevator that takes you all the way to the top where you can look out over the river—"

"Okay, okay!" Adrian held her hands up in surrender. "I get it. It's totally cool. Are you sure you haven't already been there?"

He shook his head. "Nope."

"Well, my nephews will appreciate that you're forcing me to take the afternoon off on Saturday to join them there then." She reached for the mouse again to get back to work.

He gave her a stern look and pointed at her. "Do I need to make sure you actually take the afternoon off? I don't want you to miss such an amazing experience."

"Are you trying to finagle your way into this visit?" She was teasing, but part of her wanted him to come, especially after how excited he'd grown just talking about it.

"I shouldn't interrupt your time with your family." He glanced away and then back at her with a slightly pleading expression. "Unless you just really want me there."

"Is that a puppy dog look?" She laughed.

"Maybe ..."

"Are you sure you want to hang out with a four-year-old and two-year-old? Not to mention my meddling sister."

"Sounds like a load of fun."

She shook her head. "You have no idea."

DANIELLE'S FACE, when she saw Adrian had brought a guy, was almost as good as Gray's face when he realized Adrian had a twin.

"You're identical," he whispered in her ear as if it were a huge secret.

"I know," she whispered back. "I've had twenty-six years to get used to the idea."

"Hey, Adie. Going to introduce me?" Danny walked up, her boys hanging off each hand.

"Danielle, this is Grayson Roberts, my coworker here. Gray, this is Danielle, my sister." Adrian just barely kept her balance as the boys attacked her legs. "And these are my nephews, Timmy and Seth."

Gray flashed one of his sunny smiles, and Danny raised an eyebrow so high it disappeared under her bangs. Oh, yeah. An inquisition was coming later.

They entered the outdoor paradise and wandered through the aquarium, the boys oohing and aahing over all the fish. As Gray interacted with her nephews, Adrian couldn't help but picture him as a great father, a little boy of his own with blonde hair and blue eyes. She shook the image from her head when the child in her imagination favored her a bit too.

At the barrier to the alligator marsh, Gray stood with the boys while the creatures below munched on raw chicken. Her nephews stood on their tiptoes to see, and Gray picked up Seth to have a better view. Adrian wrinkled her nose and studied the boat in the middle of the water.

Danielle pulled her back a little and gave her *the look* that meant 'spill it now, or I'll tackle you right here in public.'

"You didn't tell me you were bringing a date."

"He's not a date. He found out I was coming here and basically begged to join me because he'd always wanted to see the alligators." Adrian waved it off as if it were no big deal. "I figured you wouldn't mind."

"I don't mind. I just have a feeling you're not telling me the whole story."

Adrian gave Danielle a half glare. "Don't be ridiculous. I don't have time for anything else."

"Sometimes things happen whether you have time or not." Danielle had perfected her mom voice that said she knew best.

"Mom, come see!" Timmy waved her over and pointed to something below.

"We're not through with this conversation." Danielle went to investigate what was so interesting.

"Yes, we are."

GRAY WAS WRONG. Adrian at work wasn't the most amazing person he'd ever met. It was Adrian with children—wow! As she grabbed Seth's hand, he held the other, and they swung the boy up and out with every other step. Giggles pealed and brought smiles to everyone around.

Including Adrian.

Sure, he'd seen her smile in the last few weeks, but not like this. A real one. One that stretched across her whole face, removing the worry wrinkles between her eyes and putting a sparkle in them. *Wow.*

"You okay, there, Grayson?" Danielle smirked on his other side, Timmy holding onto her.

"It's Gray. And yes, I'm having a great time. Thanks so much for letting me crash your family gathering."

"Think nothing of it." Danielle waved her hand. "I'm always glad to meet a ... *friend* ... of my sister's."

He didn't have time to correct the false implication before Timmy pointed out another stuffed animal to go see. Not that he wanted Danielle to be wrong. On the contrary. Being here and getting a sneak peek into her family made him long to know more about her than he'd found out so far.

As tempting as it was to ask her sister, though, something told him Adrian wouldn't appreciate it at all. No. If he were going to crack through that hard exterior, he'd have to keep chiseling away a little at a time. Maybe a little more time here after her family left. Possibly dinner. Didn't food loosen tongues and open lines of communication?

It couldn't hurt to try.

And he wanted to try more than ever. So much for avoiding this at all costs.

"We've got to go meet up with Phil. I'm so glad you agreed to this today, Adie." Danny wrapped Adrian in a hug an hour later. Timmy and Seth each grabbed one of her legs.

"Me too." Adrian returned her sister's embrace and then knelt to snuggle each boy individually. She did like getting to spend time with them. Maybe in the future, she'd find more chances to take a few days off here and there so she could sneak off and play aunt.

"Adrian—" Danny pulled her aside for a moment while the boys said their goodbyes to Gray. "I know we joked about Mom and Dad not coming today, but you really should go see them again before you get too far away. Dad's ... I don't know. He just seems so much older lately than he actually is. I'm worried about him."

"And you think it's probably my fault." Adrian practically hissed.

"No." Danny shook her head. "I do think you contributed some to it, but I think it's a lot of different factors. I don't know. He won't admit anything's wrong, but I just feel like something bad is about to happen."

"I'm sure he's fine if he thinks he is. A person knows his own body better than anyone else does." Adrian didn't want to consider the alternative.

"Just think about it, okay?" Danny squeezed Adrian's arms.

"Sure. You guys be careful going home this afternoon." Adrian nodded to the boys as they ran over. "Love you guys."

"Love you too. And I do want to talk more about that other conversation we were having earlier." Danny cut her eyes in Gray's direction before looking at Adrian again.

"Too bad. There's nothing to talk about."

"I'll call you over and over and over again until you answer." Danielle batted her eyes, then grabbed her boys' hands and walked toward their minivan.

"It's still early. Want to ride up in the glass elevator to see the view?" Gray came up beside her.

Adrian leaned back and allowed her gaze to follow the contraption up, up, up to the top of the Pyramid. She didn't do heights, and that thing was high. Gray pulled a bit at her sleeve.

"Adie?" He used her family nickname.

She sent a dirty look his way. "My name is Adrian." She glanced up again.

"Not a heights person?" He followed the direction of her gaze.

"Not really."

"We don't have to, but I've heard the view is amazing. And we could check out the restaurant while we're here."

"I don't know, Gray."

"You've got to eat dinner sometime."

Adrian turned to him. "Have you been talking to my sister? That's what she said the other day when she was trying to talk me into joining them for lunch."

"Until today, I had never even met your sister. Although I probably would have recognized her anyway, seeing as you two look a lot alike." He smirked.

She laughed. "Okay. Come on. Let's go see the top of this Pyramid. But you're paying to ride the elevator."

10

Whoever decided to make a twenty-eight-story, free-standing glass elevator in this place was Adrian's worst enemy. She gripped the railing and took deep breaths, looking straight out instead of down like most of the other passengers. Gray glanced over and wrapped an arm around her shoulders, pulling her to his side without forcing her to release her grasp.

"You know this is safe, right?" he whispered.

She closed her eyes for a second before looking up at him. "In my head, yes. But for some reason, my heart just won't believe me."

Drawing her closer, he rubbed her arm with his other hand. His heart beat under her ear. The heat of his body seeped through chills she hadn't even realized she had. Her breathing eased despite the fact they still climbed. A little boy across the elevator pressed his nose to the glass and looked down. They reached the observation deck, and the door opened.

Gray took her hand and tugged her out, though not close to the edge. "Look out there."

The river sparkled in the afternoon sunshine, a silvery thread that wound its way south. To the left was downtown Memphis;

buildings, traffic. She couldn't look straight down, but the view out was pretty amazing.

"Just imagine how this would look at sunset." Gray pulled her a little farther out so he could look down. "I bet the colors would sparkle like crazy from up here."

She stared out at the river and thought he was probably right.

"If Timmy and Seth were still here, they'd probably be hanging over the railing." He pointed out to the edge of the deck.

Talk of her nephews relaxed her a bit more, although imagining them that close to the edge had her tummy flipping over. "Probably. Danny definitely has her hands full with those two."

"They're good kids." Gray grinned at her. "Want to head back and get a bite to eat?"

She glanced back at the elevator and took a shuddery breath. "I guess there's not really another way to get down?"

"Come on." He tugged her arm and led her back to wait for the elevator to return. "You've got this."

She allowed him to pull her once more into the glass deathtrap and stepped closer to him as a few other people filed in. His arm slid around her again, and he drew her even closer. Her stomach lurched as the elevator started back down, and she buried her head in his chest. She didn't have this problem on normal elevators, but with those, you couldn't see how high you were. She peeked a glance out and noticed the hanging moss and the top of the boat.

"Almost there." His whispered breath moved the hairs on the back of her neck.

What was she doing? She was much too close to this man she'd sworn wouldn't get under her skin. And yet, his arms felt safe and secure amid this insanity. Something told her she'd be wishing for this haven whenever she was unsettled from now on.

The rest of the boat came into view, and then they were on

the ground again. He kept his arm around her as they walked back out into the store. She leaned back and stared up at where they'd been moments before.

"Just twenty-eight stories. Not so bad, right?" he asked.

She shook her head. "I shouldn't have let you talk me into that. Now I've completely humiliated myself."

"Being scared of heights isn't humiliating. Don't worry. I still think you're impressive."

It dawned on her, she was still wrapped up in his arms. She stepped away and motioned around. "So, dinner?"

His hand found the small of her back, and he led her to the restaurant. Normally something like that would drive her crazy, but today it felt nice. He wasn't pushing, just letting a gentle touch lead the way. In the restaurant, he pulled her chair out for her and then sat down.

"Thanks for letting me tag along today. I know it must have taken a lot of trust to let me see that much of your personal life." He glanced at her from over his menu.

"Look, I know I don't open up much. I admit I'm not an easy person to get to know. I just—well, I've been burned in the past too many times to really want to make friends anymore. It's too painful." She fiddled with the napkin-wrapped silverware.

The waitress came and took their drink orders, saving her from having to explain, but something told her he wouldn't let her off very easily.

"Sometimes it's worth a little pain to be able to enjoy all the good that comes with it." He contemplated his menu as if it held all the secrets to life.

Though her mind wasn't on what to eat, she picked hers up and perused it enough to find something that sounded good. She wanted to argue with him, but how could she unless she told him more of her past? He'd already accessed too many of the walls she kept up around her heart.

Her phone buzzed, and she checked it. Caller ID said *Danny*. She hit *ignore* and set the phone aside again. Her sister hadn't wasted any time calling to talk more. The boys must be asleep in the car on the way back, so she figured she could have an adult conversation without them interrupting to talk to Aunt Adie.

She looked at Gray and found him studying her. "I know you want to know more about me, but it's complicated. I'm not sure you'd understand."

"TRY ME." Gray leaned forward, wishing he could pull out of her what caused that frown in the middle of her forehead.

Adrian wrapped and unwrapped a straw paper around her finger. "I don't know where to start."

"Start with the basics." Gray took the paper away and touched her fingers. "Tell me about your family. Where are you from? Where did you grow up? Where's home?"

"Home." The word practically spat from her mouth. "I don't guess I really have one. Everyone wants to know where someone is from, but in my case, that's probably one of the most complicated parts."

"Everyone has a home." He frowned.

She shook her head. "We moved around a lot. The longest I ever lived somewhere was about six years, but usually it was more like two to four years."

"Military?" Relaxing back in his chair, he hoped it would relax her enough to talk, too.

She paused. Would she finally open up?

"Preacher. My dad is a preacher. And after you move around so many times, you quit considering any of the places home. They're just places you lived for a while. You can't put down roots when you're only planted in the top layer of the soil."

"You'd be surprised what you can do when you're only planted in the top layer of the soil." He leaned forward again.

"How would you know?" Bitterness laced her voice. "Are you a preacher's kid too?"

The urge to tell her his backstory niggled in his gut, but he pushed it aside. Now was not the time. "No. But you still might be amazed at what all I know."

Her phone buzzed again. She hit *ignore* with a huff of annoyance. She must want to talk to him if she didn't grab the excuse of a phone call to get out of it.

"Is that Brad?" Gray pointed to the device.

"No. It's my sister. She threatened to call me until I told her something, but I can ignore her just as long as she can continue to press redial. We're twins. We have the same stubbornness."

Reaching over, he took her hands. "Listen, Adrian. I'm not saying that I understand everything you went through growing up. My dad isn't a preacher. I didn't have the same experiences. I'm just saying maybe you should give me a chance."

Please, God, show me how to help her.

BEFORE ADRIAN COULD REPLY, her phone beeped with a text message.

> Adie, answer your phone. It's about Dad.

As it started buzzing again, she snatched it up. "Danny? What's going on?"

"Dad's in the hospital. He had a heart attack."

Gray must have picked up on the fact that something was wrong. By the time Adrian hung up with her sister, he'd loaded their food in to-go containers and was paying the bill.

She pointed to the receipt. "You didn't have to pay for my dinner."

"Call it recompense for the earlier trauma I put you through when I dragged you to the top of the Pyramid." He folded his wallet and slid it back into his pocket.

"I've got to go. Which you obviously already realized." She motioned to their food. "My dad is in the hospital."

"Let's go." He picked up their dinner and walked with her out of the store.

Had it been only five hours ago that they walked up and met Danielle and the boys? It seemed like much longer.

"Is there anything I can do to help?" Gray asked as they wove through the Saturday evening traffic.

She drummed her fingers on the steering wheel as they came to a stop for a moment. "No. I just need to grab a few things, and then I'll head to Arkansas tonight. Sassafras is only a couple hours away. I'll be back Monday in time for work."

"You don't have to do that. It sounded like things were pretty serious with your dad." Gray leaned forward until he caught her eye. "Take the time you need, and we'll make it without you. Brad is just a phone call away, and he should be able to talk me through whatever comes up until you get back."

"We're just over a week out from going live. I won't abandon you now. I'll be back Monday." She clenched and unclenched her jaw. "Besides, I discovered several years ago that I can't stay around my family for very long without things blowing up anyway."

He didn't say anything, but she could sense him studying her. She pulled into the hotel parking lot and into the spot beside his car. Before she could take her food and run inside, he caught her arm.

"Promise me that if you need to stay, you will. Family is important. I don't want you to regret coming back earlier than you should have." His voice was serious, tinged with something that sounded like regret. It made her wish they could have continued the conversation they'd had at the restaurant.

"I'll see you Monday." She'd reiterate her point until he finally believed it if it took all night. Which she didn't have.

"Unless you don't." His gaze held hers. "Which will be fine too."

She wanted to argue more but decided their stubbornness was evenly matched for the moment. Instead, she just quoted her teenage self. "Sure, whatever."

He seemed to accept that. "I'll pray for your safety and for your dad. Call me if you need anything, okay?"

A big part of her wanted to launch herself into those arms that had felt so safe earlier on the elevator. Her life was plummeting just as fast right now, and there was nothing to hold on to. But she couldn't.

Instead, she ran up to her room, threw a few items in a duffel, and hit the road once more.

That evening, as she drove across east Arkansas, her phone buzzed. She pushed the Bluetooth button on her steering wheel.

"Hello?"

"Adrian, it's Brad."

She'd meant to call him while she was packing earlier, but she'd spent the time stewing over her conversation with Gray instead.

"Grayson called me and filled me in on your situation," Brad said in a no-nonsense voice.

"What?" Adrian couldn't believe Gray's audacity. How dare he butt into her personal business?

"Don't worry. Gray and I worked out a plan in case it takes you longer than the rest of the weekend. Just go be with your family. I already felt bad that your vacation time was cut short, anyway. Keep Gray and me updated, and don't worry about work. We've got your back."

Adrian's knuckles were white on the steering wheel as she drove farther from a man who'd gotten under her skin so much this afternoon. She couldn't think of anyone she wasn't related to who'd chipped away at her privacy fence. He was way too close. It was good she was headed away from him for at least a day or two. She might just stay longer than she'd planned if only to avoid seeing Grayson Roberts for an extra twenty-four hours.

VISITING hours were over when Adrian made it to town. She considered finding a motel room for the night instead of going to the house, but she was there to be with her family whether she liked it or not. She drove down the quiet streets and pulled in behind her sister's van.

Danny came out the carport door and wrapped her in a fierce hug.

"You did just see me a few hours ago." Adrian gave a playful smile. She hoped by teasing, the whole situation would seem less sober. Instead, it emphasized the seriousness.

"That doesn't make me any less glad to see you now." Danny nodded toward the house. "Mom finally gave up and went to bed. We had to drag her home from the hospital. She wanted to stay with him, but we convinced her they'd both get more rest if she came with us."

"How is he?" Adrian slowly walked beside her sister up the drive.

"Tired. Frustrated. Angry at himself because he thinks he 'let it happen.'" Danny kicked at an old ball that was in her path in the carport. "It's going to be ridiculous convincing him to rest and recover from this. He's trying to figure out how he can preach in the morning."

"Preaching's probably part of what caused this in the first place. It's got to be one of the most stressful jobs in the world." Adrian went through the backdoor and waved to Phil sitting at the kitchen counter.

Danny stepped past her and picked up a half-full glass of tea. "Maybe. I'm just glad it wasn't a major heart attack. But he has to be more careful from here on out. A little more exercise. Eat better. Try to keep at least some of the stresses down in his life."

Ignoring the pointed look her sister shot her way, Adrian wouldn't go down this road tonight. She was here to support, not fight. Instead, she carried her bag to her room, and when she came back, Danny handed her a glass of tea.

Adrian sat beside Phil and took a sip. "So, what happened? I mean, I know he had a heart attack, but were there signs or anything? He looked okay a couple weeks ago." Actually, thinking back on it, he'd appeared fatigued then. She'd simply brushed it off because she didn't want to face facts. Still didn't want to.

"I told you he'd been looking worn down. Mom said he's been staying busier than ever. She said it's the way he copes with things he doesn't want to think about. He seems to think if he can just stay busy enough, he won't have time to think about things he can't fix." Danny shot her another look, and Adrian pursed her lips to keep from saying something she might regret.

Why all the sudden reminders of how Adrian was a disappointment to her whole family? She was here, wasn't she?

"Anyway, evidently, he's been organizing the local preachers' luncheons, attending Rotary Club meetings, volunteering at the food bank, and had three funerals in the last month on top of writing sermons and other normal stuff."

Adrian thought about all the things she took on and did for work to keep from thinking about things. Possibly because she was so much like Dad in some ways. Growing up, she had such a close relationship with him.

Danny leaned back against the counter. "Mom said he just collapsed at the breakfast table this morning. No warnings or anything. She called 911 and followed him to the hospital. They were afraid it was a stroke, but he's been able to talk and move everything like normal. It could have been a lot worse."

"But you didn't call me until this evening. Why didn't Mom call us this morning?" Adrian rolled her empty glass around in front of her.

"Danny's phone was buried in her purse, and mine was on silent." Phil glanced up from his laptop where he'd been typing something. "She couldn't get ahold of us."

"My phone was in my pocket, and she never called me."

No one said anything.

So that's how it was going to be the rest of the weekend. Maybe she should have stayed in Memphis.

Adrian stood up and put her glass in the sink. "I guess I'll head to bed. I'll go visit Dad in the morning."

"What about church?" Danny asked.

"I came to see Dad. That's why I'm here. No other reason." Adrian walked down the hall to wash her face. She could hear Danny and Phil talking quietly in their room as she closed the door to hers. What would it be like to have someone to support her in a situation like this? To hold her when she just wanted to cry because everything seemed to be falling apart all of a sudden?

The scent of Gray's cologne wafted through the air as she pulled her shirt over her head. It must have transferred to the fabric while they were on the elevator. She held it to her nose and breathed it in. He would've come with her if she'd asked. He'd acted more in the last week like he might be interested in being more than coworkers, maybe even more than friends. What would it be like to have him here?

She shook her head and dropped her top on the desk chair. Temporary assignment, remember? Besides, he would've insisted she go to church services in the morning.

11

Adrian kissed Mom's cheek the next morning before she slipped out the back door. She didn't even wait for a cup of coffee. Danielle had been feeding the boys waffles at the table, and Phil was in the shower. This was her best shot at leaving without further conflict.

Driving through the still-sleepy streets, she made her way to the north side of town to the hospital. She'd been inside only once before, when she came with Dad to visit one of the church members. Today she walked through the sliding doors alone and asked at the desk where her father's room was. The halls were quiet this early in the morning, and the sound of her shoes echoed as she followed the directions.

"Two-twenty B." Not that one. Ah. There. "Two-twenty C." Should she knock? She didn't want to wake him.

The room was dark when she pushed open the door and slipped inside. His snore was quieter than normal, probably because of the oxygen tubes in his nose. She silently lowered herself into the chair beside his bed. Not wanting to steal from his rest, she pulled out a book she'd brought just in case.

Even with a book from one of her favorite authors, her attention waned. She studied her father. He appeared older than he had even a few weeks before, his cheeks a little sallower, his thinning hair mussed on top. Did she even know what to say when he woke up?—no. She just needed to be here. Out the window was a small garden, birds flying back and forth, cotton fields across the highway.

A nurse came in to check her dad's blood pressure and temperature. He stirred and looked over at Adrian. Their eyes held for a moment before he returned his attention to the nurse. Her dad shifted to sit up a bit more as the nurse slipped out of the room.

"I see you're sticking to your beliefs this morning." He raised an eyebrow at her.

She returned his stare without wavering. "Good morning to you too. How are you feeling?"

"The usual. More worried about you than myself."

"I'm doing fine. You're the one who just had a heart attack." Adrian pointed at him.

"But my illness is just physical. Yours goes beyond that. A, don't you think it's time we talked?"

Adrian stood. "I haven't had any coffee yet. Do you want anything from the cafeteria?"

He seemed about to say something, then shook his head. "I'm sure the nurse will bring whatever the doctor has deemed me fit to eat this morning."

Time to make an exit before he could change his mind. Her legs ate up the hallway as she headed to the other end of the hospital. *What's wrong with everybody? Isn't this a free country? Can't I be mad at God without it being such a big deal? Haven't I earned the right to make my own decisions? I didn't even have to come. I could've stayed in Memphis.*

Grabbing a Styrofoam cup, she filled it with steamy black coffee. A liberal dosing of sugar and creamer and a twirl of the swizzle stick turned it a perfect light brown. With the lid carefully pressed on, she handed some money to the cashier and meandered back toward her father's room. How could she make him understand? This visit wasn't supposed to be about her. It was about him. She'd turn the focus back where it should be.

When she returned, he had a tray in front of him.

"Broth for breakfast." He shook his head and pushed the liquid around with a spoon. "Not what I would've enjoyed at home."

"They were having waffles." She took a sip of coffee as she reclaimed her chair.

He dropped the spoon onto his tray and leaned back. "Rub it in, why don't you?"

She smirked. This was more like the dad she used to know. He picked up his grape popsicle and took a bite instead.

"So how serious was this? I mean, Danny made it sound like it wasn't too bad, but I thought she might be trying to cushion the blow or something. Are you really okay?" Adrian crossed her legs and blew on her beverage before taking another sip.

"I'm fine. It was more a scare than anything. I could probably go preach this morning if they'd sign the papers saying I could leave here." He rubbed a hand over his bald spot and messed his hair up even worse.

"Dad, you don't just jump back from a heart attack, even a minor one. If the doctor thinks you need some time off, you need to listen."

"Your mother thinks I need to start exercising more. She's talking about joining a class at the senior center. We're not old enough to join the senior center. I also don't want to think about trying to join the same class as some of those old ladies from church." He made a face, and she had to laugh with him as she imagined the widows in their sweatsuits and headbands.

He pointed to the table beside her. "Can you hand me my Bible? Since I can't be with the church this morning physically, I want to at least join them mentally."

The leather was soft as she passed it to him. His fingers caressed the cover before he opened the pages and found what he was looking for. He adjusted his glasses and leaned back to read.

As she finished her coffee, she studied the room. Four different vases with flower arrangements lined the windowsill. Above one of them hovered a balloon that said, *Get Well Soon*. She turned her head sideways and read one of the cards poking out—from one of the church ladies.

"We have a great church family here." Dad's voice pulled her away from her snooping.

She jerked her head up and looked back at him.

"I know you don't believe it's possible, but we do. They love us, and they love you, too, even though they haven't seen you in a few years. As soon as word got around that I was here yesterday, those flowers and calls and cards started arriving. They're faster than the post office."

"They're pretty flowers." She chose to comment on the part of his words she was most comfortable with.

He went back to his reading, so she picked up her book and tried to focus on it for a while. When she couldn't concentrate for more than three words in a row, she gave up and pulled out her laptop. Maybe working on a problem that hadn't been fixed Friday afternoon would hold her attention better.

A couple of hours later, the quiet was interrupted as Timmy and Seth pushed the door open. Adrian slipped out to find another cup of coffee as the rest of her family filed in. Danny reached out to her, but Adrian ducked her head and hastened down the hall.

"Are you eating lunch with us, Aunt Adie?" Timmy pulled on her leg the moment she stepped back into her dad's room.

"I don't know, Timmy. I thought I might hang out with Grandpa a bit more before I have to go back to Memphis this evening."

He stuck his lip out and gave her a pouty face. "But don't you want to hang out with me?"

"I hung out with you all afternoon yesterday. How about you give some other people a turn?" Adrian ruffled his hair.

"We'll be back after lunch." Mom gave her arm a squeeze as she walked by. "Do you want us to bring you anything?"

Adrian shrugged. "A sandwich might be good. You know what I like." She met Dad's gaze as she resumed her seat. "What?"

"It's not nice to use me to get out of spending time with your nephew."

"I didn't 'use' you." She used air quotes to emphasize the word. "I did come to see you. And I did spend time with him yesterday."

He was quiet for a few moments before speaking again. "Did you want to come? Or was it more of an obligation?"

"I didn't *want* to come because you had a heart attack. And, yes, there are some obligations that come with being a family. But I wasn't forced to come this weekend, if that's what you're asking. I needed to see that you're really okay."

He gave her a very serious look. "What if I wasn't okay?"

"But you said you were."

"But A, what if I hadn't been okay? What if this had been more serious and I had gone on to meet my maker?"

She shook her head. What was he talking about? "I still would've come. I just would've had to pack a black dress."

"You're not listening."

"I am listening." She stood up and paced the few feet from the chair to the window and back. "You're asking me if I'd have come if you'd died. Yes. I would've come. You're my father."

"No. I'm asking you how you would've handled things if I hadn't been okay." He tilted his head as his eyes followed her path back and forth across the small room.

"I don't know." She held her hands out. "I probably won't know until it happens. But I'm glad it hasn't happened yet. I don't want to lose you."

"Then why do you keep pushing me away?"

She perched on the edge of the chair, her hands loosely

clasped in front of her. "I'm not pushing you away. You and mom make me feel like I'm some sort of pariah. I'm twenty-six years old. I'm old enough to make my own decisions even if they're not the ones you want me to make. Daddy, I'm doing okay."

He touched his steepled fingers to his forehead, almost as if he were praying. When he met her gaze again, his eyes were sad.

"I wonder all the time. I wonder what I did wrong, if I could've said something different, or said something I didn't say, if I could've done one thing instead of another. I was so focused —so sure God wanted me to preach, I forgot that my more important job was to be a daddy.

"I think, maybe if I hadn't been so selfish, maybe if I hadn't continued to pursue this job I love, I could've saved the soul of the daughter I love. Because no matter how many souls I'm able to save by continuing to preach, if I've lost yours, I've failed beyond compare." A tear traced its way down his cheek.

Adrian felt tears of her own welling in her eyes. "Daddy—" How could she put in words she didn't blame him for her anger at God?

The door pushed open and one of the church elders stuck his head in. "Preacher? How ya doing?"

His wife followed him into the room and smiled at Adrian. "Where are those boys of yours, Danielle? I enjoyed having Seth in class this morning."

"I'm Adrian, actually. Everyone else went to get lunch." She rose from the chair and grabbed her bag. "I need some fresh air, Dad. I'll be back in a bit."

The look he gave her said he wished they could have continued their conversation. She didn't want to leave with him feeling so guilty, but she couldn't tell him everything with other people in the room. Maybe she'd get more alone time with him before she headed back to Memphis this evening.

"HOW'S YOUR FRIEND?" Victoria caught Gray after worship Sunday morning. "Adrian, right?"

Just hearing her name did something to his stomach now, and he had to swallow a lump before he could answer. "She's actually in Arkansas today. Her Dad had a heart attack."

"Oh no!" Christine joined the conversation. "Does she need anything? What can we do on top of praying?"

"I'm not sure, actually." Gray rubbed the back of his neck. "She's planning to come back this evening."

"I'm game for a road trip if you want to try and head over there to show support." Nathan clasped his shoulder from the other side of the girls. "Sorry. Couldn't help but overhear."

"That's a great idea." Victoria nodded. "Wait. What part of Arkansas?"

"Sassafras?" Gray sifted through the mush that was his brain. "I think she said it was a couple hours from here."

"Perfect." Nathan rubbed his hands. "We can all go change into more comfortable clothes, grab a quick bite, and be on our way."

"You really want to do this?" Gray looked at the faces of his friends. Proof that Adrian was wrong about people at church not caring about you. Maybe this was exactly what she needed to see.

"Of course we do." Christine slung her purse over her shoulder. "We had fun getting to spend time with her at the banquet and would love to get to know her more. Besides, she seems like she needs a church family, and if this opens some doors, even better."

Christine had no idea, but Gray was glad he wasn't the only one thinking along those lines. "Okay. Meet back here around one?"

"It's a plan, Brother." Nathan nodded.

Gray let his parents know what was going on, and they quickly agreed this was more important than him eating lunch with them like normal. He changed in record time and threw

95

together a peanut butter sandwich. Best source of protein he could think of in a hurry.

He had to admit, he'd quit trying to push Adrian away as much. Who was he kidding? Yesterday he'd literally pulled her to him. And enjoyed it.

Somehow knowing she'd been a Christian once had given him hope. Not only for her but also for something more between the two of them. And if God chose to use him to help her find her way back, he'd gladly be a vessel.

He didn't expect to be the reason she came back to God. She'd have to do that on her own. But he knew from personal experience how much being surrounded by a good church family could work towards softening a heart. It was one of the reasons he was a Christian today.

As he pulled up how to get from Memphis to Sassafras, a niggle of doubt ran through his head. Would Adrian be angry at him for intruding into her family life? Besides yesterday, they'd kept everything fairly business. Nothing too personal. How she reacted when they walked in could determine where they went from here on out.

His fingers shook a bit as he hit the button to pull up the map. Only one way to find out.

THE CONVERSATION with Dad left Adrian's insides roiling. As far back as she could remember, she'd wanted to make Dad proud.

'Just do the best you can do, and I'll be happy,' he'd always told her, but she wanted to do even better. That's why she'd studied so hard to maintain all As through school, had memorized hundreds of Bible verses as a child, had worked to build up this job so she could support herself. But it wasn't enough.

She flopped onto one of the plastic-covered armchairs in the family waiting area near her dad's room, close enough to be easily found but not in the midst of everything. She leaned her head back against the wall and closed her eyes for a minute. It was a hard pill to swallow to know she wouldn't be able to make Dad completely proud.

But that was part of her problem the last few years. She'd disappointed him even though he felt he was the one who'd let her down instead.

Danny found her a little later and handed her a sandwich before returning to be with the rest of the family. Several people whom Adrian recognized as being members of Dad's congregation walked by throughout the afternoon. 'We have a great church family here,' Dad had said. She wanted to believe such things existed. Especially since she'd met some of Gray's, too, and they seemed really nice.

As if her thoughts had conjured him, Gray appeared in front of her out of nowhere. "I thought you came to see your dad."

"Gray, what are you doing here?" She jumped to her feet. "How did you find me?" A tornado of emotions ripped through her—surprise, frustration, excitement. And then it settled. As agitated as she'd been with him the evening before, his presence had a soothing effect on her troubled spirit.

"You mentioned Sassafras, Arkansas, yesterday as your destination, so I looked it up."

"And you just decided to come? Why?" Before Adrian could form a complete sentence, Victoria, Christine, and Nathan joined them.

"We wanted to support you." Gray motioned to the others. "They were asking me about you at church this morning, so I told them about your dad. We all decided just to grab a sandwich and come be with you this afternoon, see if your family needed anything."

"That's a two-hour drive!" Adrian tried to wrap her mind around something she never would've considered a possibility.

"Adrian, did you—" Danny came around the corner and stopped short.

"Hi, Danny." Gray waved.

"Gray, I wasn't expecting to see you." Danny's focus ricocheted from him to Adrian and back again before moving on to the others.

"We wanted to come support Adrian." He quickly made introductions.

"You were asking a question when you came in." Adrian grabbed her sister's attention again before she could start digging into more personal matters.

"Oh." Danny put a finger to her lips as she thought. "I can't even remember what I was asking. Something Mom wanted to know."

"I'll go see what she wants."

Danny looked at the others. "You guys are more than welcome to come meet our dad too. I'm sure he'd be pleased to know some of Adrian's friends." The way she said it made it sound like Adrian didn't have friends.

And I don't really.

Gray's hand hovered at the small of her back as they walked down the hall. Had it only been the day before when he'd first done that? The slight pressure was comforting. How had he known she'd wanted him here even though she hadn't admitted it until she saw him?

As everyone filed in, her parents glanced up from a conversation. Phil must have gone home to put the boys down for a nap since they were nowhere to be seen. The other church members had also gone. Mom squeezed her dad's hand and stood.

What was the best way to introduce everyone? She was at a loss. "Dad, this is Grayson Roberts. I'm working with him right now at Healthcare for All in Memphis."

Gray stepped forward and shook Dad's hand with one of his warmest smiles. "It's a pleasure to meet you, sir. I'm enjoying getting to know your daughter."

"It's a pleasure to meet you." Dad raised an eyebrow. "I'm James Stewart—the preacher, not the actor."

The obligatory laugh fell easily from Gray's mouth. And she knew, because he was that kind of guy, he meant it. It wasn't only to make Dad happy.

"This is Christine, Victoria, and Nathan. They all worship with the same congregation I do." Since Gray took the introductions away, Adrian didn't have to worry as much about how to explain their relationship to her. "They met Adrian last weekend when I bullied her into singing with us."

Adrian avoided her family's looks. She knew how shocked they probably were without seeing it for herself. Instead, she watched the little green line as it bounced across the screen with each one of Dad's heartbeats.

"We came to support Adrian." Gray squeezed her shoulder. "But we'd love to pray with you. That you recover quickly and get to resume life outside the hospital."

"That would be great." Dad contemplated Adrian again, but she looked away. The questions would come fast and hard once she was alone with her family again. And she wasn't sure how to answer them.

Gray grabbed her hand and Dad's. Everyone else in the room joined in until they formed a circle. Adrian fought back guilt and something else as everyone else bowed their heads.

"Father God, we come to You this afternoon to ask blessings on this family." Gray's voice was fervent, and he squeezed her hand as he continued. "We know You send rain on the just and unjust, and right now that rain is falling on the Stewart family. We ask that You heal Mr. Stewart, return him to his normal health so that he can continue in his work to spread the word of Your love.

"Please be with his family as they worry about him and help them to remember that he's in Your hands. Be with the doctors as they use their knowledge to help him have better health. And please be with Adrian as she travels back to us in Memphis and keep her safe. We thank You so much for listening to our prayers. In Jesus' name, amen."

The situation was completely out of Adrian's hands. Before she could say another word, Nathan and Gray were chatting with her father, the girls with her sister and mother, and she was standing there wondering if anything today was real. After about half an hour, another couple who worshipped with her parents walked in. Adrian recognized the man as being another one of the elders.

"Hey, Brother. We didn't realize you were having so many visitors this afternoon. Just came to check and see what all you needed." He came over and shook Dad's hand.

"I think we're doing okay. The doctors said I should be able to go home again tomorrow, assuming all goes well the rest of today and tonight." Dad did look much better than he had this morning. What had changed? Was it that he'd been able to eat a little more than broth for lunch? Was it all the visits he'd received?

As Adrian pondered the changes, the elder continued talking with her dad. "Don't worry about anything. We had your pulpit covered today, and we can do it as long as we need until the doctors say you're ready to jump back up there. We want you healthy enough to be able to preach for a long time. Some of us may not be as eloquent as you, but we'll suffice until you're back on your feet."

Adrian blinked. The elders were basically her dad's boss. In some of the places they'd lived, those elders frowned if her father had to miss even one service for being sick. They'd been aggravated if her family wanted to take a vacation, or visit relatives in another state and be gone over the weekend. These men were offering to wait for her dad as long as they needed. Gray caught her eye and gave her a questioning look as if to ask if she were all right. She wasn't sure.

12

Adrian walked bleary-eyed into work the next morning. Even though she returned to Memphis early enough, she fought sleep most of the night. Before she left the hospital, her father squeezed her hands in his and told her he wasn't as worried about her anymore and that he liked her new friends. Conversations from the whole weekend replayed in her head until the early morning hours.

"Good morning." Gray glanced up at her only a moment before looking back at his computer. He clicked his mouse quickly, probably helping someone else fix a problem on their computer through a shared screen. She pulled out her laptop and dropped her bag beside her chair.

"You ready for our meeting in a few minutes?" Gray interrupted her as she was skimming emails.

She spun her chair around to face him, and her knees knocked into his. "Sorry. What meeting?"

"Please tell me I told you we have a meeting this morning." Gray looked sheepish. "Didn't I?"

"If you did, I forgot about it."

"Don't worry. It's nothing major. We'll go over basic things— make sure all the problems we've found have been fixed, and figure out what scenarios still need to be run before next Thursday. Then we'll make sure everyone knows their part and probably talk about who will work on the weekend of the Fourth."

She nodded. "I was already figuring on working that weekend. Most people get to take holidays, but I don't when it's only a few days after rolling out a new software program."

"No one is working that whole weekend. We'll take shifts. You've trained us all well enough that even if something happens, one of the IT guys can keep things going until you or I can get here to work through it. And we'll have the support of your IT staff in St. Louis too." The warmth of his knee pressed against hers began to mess with her head.

"I'm not on your staff. I'm on Brad's staff. I'll be here. Trust me. That's how it should be." She stood and stepped away a bit, so she wasn't touching him anymore. "Do I have time to get some coffee before the meeting?"

"Sure. We've got another fifteen minutes."

She inhaled deeply as she poured the black liquid into a cup. Even the scent of it helped revive her senses. She stirred in flavored creamer and took a sip to see if she could wake up even more. She never had problems like she'd faced this training session. What was going on?

Gray walked beside her to the conference room upstairs several minutes later. There was no mention of anything that had happened over the weekend. Nor did he put his hand on the small of her back. She missed it.

"My dad is supposed to be released today." Maybe bringing the subject up would ease some of the tension she was dealing with even though he seemed to be his normal self.

"That's great, Adrian. Your family seems awesome."

"Dad thought you guys were pretty great too." She cut a glance in his direction.

He shrugged. "We just did what any Christian would do."

"No." She shook her head. "Not every Christian acts like you do."

She entered the conference room before he could argue with her. The meeting stretched on through the morning. Adrian tried to pay attention but kept stealing glances at Gray. So much had happened over the last few days, and yet he acted as though everything were the same. Was it the same for him? Had she only imagined the importance of him driving to Arkansas?

Brad joined the discussion via teleconference, and she made notes of everything he suggested they test this week. She'd have her hands full with all these trial runs. Maybe working hard would help keep her mind off other things. Not that it had done a great job the last few weeks.

"We're rolling this out next Thursday, right?" The sound of Brad's papers flipping back and forth came through the speaker.

"Right." Gray leaned forward to be heard a little better through the phone. "We'll go live on the first."

"Great. That gives us just a couple days before the holiday weekend. If your company is anything like some others we've worked with in the past, holiday weekends are crazy anyway. Do a lot of your health care providers take off or work off-schedule?"

One of the office managers answered. "Yes. I've already got some people scheduled to work extra shifts that weekend. I'm hoping if we all stay on top of things as they happen, maybe it will go a little more smoothly."

Brad murmured his agreement and then offered a few other suggestions. "Adrian, what are your plans for that weekend?"

"I'm here, Brad. I'll be here as long as they need me." She caught Gray staring at her with an expression she couldn't quite read. She quickly returned her focus to the meeting as Brad continued to talk.

"Great. I'll have a few extra guys here that weekend, too, to help with any unforeseen problems that might pop up. But it sounds like you're coming across very few issues as you run these scenarios, so I'll take that as a good sign. Maybe we'll all get to leave early on the Fourth and go see some fireworks."

Fireworks. Honestly, if they made it through the holiday without some big mishap or another—or even ten little ones— Adrian would count it as a success, and that would be celebration enough. She couldn't remember the last time she got to see the yearly pyrotechnics most Americans seemed to love. She straightened her stack of papers and threw away her cup.

"Would you like to go grab lunch?" Gray fell into step with her as they returned to their office.

"I'll probably grab something later." She held up her notebook. "I need to get at least one of these scenarios set up to run so I can see what it looks like when I get back."

He grabbed her arm and gently steered her around a trash can in the middle of the floor catching drips from the leaky ceiling. She clutched the notebook to her chest where it wouldn't keep her from seeing further obstacles, not that she was complaining about an excuse for him to touch her. She could still feel the pressure of his hand on her forearm even though he'd put his hands back in his pockets.

Ugh. What was wrong with her? What happened to all her walls? Those didn't include touching.

"Have you had anything besides coffee today?" His voice echoed off the stairwell as they made their way down.

"You're worse than my mom." She pushed open the door. "No. I haven't had anything besides coffee."

"Let's get this scenario running, then, and go grab a sandwich. You look exhausted, and some protein will help you get through the afternoon."

"Who did you take care of before I came? Do you babysit everyone you work with or just people you share an office space with?" The questions came out harsher than she meant for them to, but her confusion was messing with her temper.

He held his hands up as if in surrender. "Sorry. I didn't realize

I was coddling you. I'll go grab a sandwich alone and be back later."

"Gray—"

He turned back to look at her in the doorway.

"I'm sorry." She placed her notebook on her desk. "You're right. I'm exhausted. And I do need to eat. I'm just trying to stay professional because I feel like I've been slacking on this job, and that's not me. I never slack."

"I believe that." He hovered in the doorway another moment before walking into the office. "But I also know you haven't been slacking here either. Things are going great. Even Brad thought we'd all be able to leave early on the Fourth. Stop worrying so much, and trust that things are under control, even if it's not *your* control. God has this."

She barely kept herself from rolling her eyes. Why did God have to be brought into this? Couldn't this man have a single conversation without bringing Him into it?

"Can I help you get this scenario running and then take you to lunch?" He sat on the edge of his chair.

She nodded. "Okay. Fine. Let's get this thing running so you can quit worrying about me." She shot him a half-smile to show she was mostly teasing.

***

AN HOUR LATER, Gray sat across from her at a local Tex-Mex restaurant. "You keep telling me I wouldn't understand your story and that it's too long to tell. What if we just do a little bit each day?"

"Why is it so important to you to learn my story?" She took a bite of taco and then wiped her chin.

"You intrigue me." He popped a chip in his mouth and chewed for a moment. "And I love a good challenge, so when you told me I wouldn't understand, I wanted to see if you're right."

She shook her head. "I'm not intriguing."

"I think you are." He pointed at her with his burrito. "And that's all that matters."

"If you say so." She took a sip of her tea and thought. "I wouldn't know where to start."

"Most people start at the beginning of a story, right? Why not just tell me a little bit about the early years, and we'll slowly inch our way through high school by the end of the week?"

She wrinkled her nose. "I didn't even like high school when I was in it."

"It's just a thought." He shrugged.

Adrian pursed her lips. "I don't remember much about my youngest years. I know we moved about five times between when I was born and when I was in the third grade. I have a faint memory of playing in certain rooms in some of the houses, how the furniture was arranged, and the toys we had. But as to events, I don't remember much. Little kids are resilient, you know?"

"I do know." Boy, did he ever know. He probably shouldn't be as emotionally healthy today as he was, but God had blessed him tremendously with his parents and church family. Otherwise, he might've turned out much worse.

Maybe after he lured out her past with food each day, he could let her hear his story too. He wasn't ashamed of it or anything. But he didn't talk about it much either. He'd moved on. Now he prayed he could help her do the same.

———

EACH DAY that week he showed her a different place to eat, and each time she talked about a few more years of her past.

Over burgers, "Elementary school wasn't too bad. Even though kids are sort of judgmental, it doesn't really kick in until middle and high school. So I could make friends in first and second grade. When my 'boyfriend' found out I was moving at the end of the school year in third grade, though, he broke up with me. I was devastated."

"You had a boyfriend in third grade?" Gray gave her a look of disbelief. He should not be jealous of a third-grade boyfriend. And yet ...

"The teacher let us sit in desks right next to each other, and sometimes he would reach over and hold my hand. It was all very romantic." She smiled at the memory. "His name was Jimmy."

"Obviously one of the better memories."

"Until he broke up with me." She ate a French fry. "That was, I think, the first time I really realized how moving so much affected my life. Even if I made friends, I had to leave them again. We said we'd write each other and stay friends always, but that never lasts long. Out of sight, out of mind."

"I can't imagine someone putting you out of their mind that easily." The words slipped easily from his lips. Because he knew he'd never forget her.

At a salad bar the next day, "For fourth and fifth grade, I still tried to fit in. We didn't have much money. Preachers don't get paid a lot. At least not at the little congregations my dad likes to work with. I remember wanting this pair of black wedge sandals. All the other girls in my class had some. But we just didn't have the money at the time."

"But the kids at church were nicer, right?" Gray broke off a piece of breadstick and munched it while he listened.

She drew a pattern through her leftover dressing. "Sort of, but not really. They would let me sit with them if I asked, but they never invited me. And my dad was teaching our Sunday school class for a while right around then, so they all expected me and Danny to know all the answers.

"Of course, when I worked on our lessons at home and would ask Dad for the answers, he'd tell me I could figure it out and point to the passage in the Bible I was supposed to be reading. I used to think he didn't care if I got it right or not—that he would've helped the other kids in our class if they'd asked."

"He probably just wanted you to learn it and knew you'd figure it out if you read the scripture."

"I had read the scripture!" Her voice was loaded with hurt, and she grimaced. "Sorry. I didn't realize I was still so upset about this. But I had read it. I just couldn't find exactly what the lesson was asking for. And he didn't have time to help me."

Gray pointed at her with his fork. "I met your dad. I can't imagine him not wanting to help you, Adrian. Maybe that's what fourth-grade you thought, but do you actually think it's true?"

HER DAD'S words from Sunday had continued to run through her head all week. *"No matter how many souls I'm able to save by continuing to preach, if I've lost yours, I have failed beyond compare."*

Thursday, Gray changed things up. Over egg rolls and sweet and sour chicken, he asked, "Why did you guys move so much?"

She chewed a bite of egg roll before answering. "I don't even really know. I know a couple of times Dad left because he thought where we were living wasn't a good place for us. The schools weren't very good, and he wanted better for us when we were in kindergarten. I think I heard him say that one place didn't have any elders and the men kept fighting with each other as they tried to make decisions. It just wasn't a good situation."

"That makes sense. He wanted to keep you guys safe and give you the best he could."

She nodded. "I know there was one time Dad was asked to leave because he'd been preaching through Matthew, and the congregation protested when he did some lessons on marriage and divorce. He was simply telling them what the Bible said, but several of them had been divorced and remarried and didn't like it."

"So it wasn't his fault. He was preaching the truth, and the people didn't want to hear it." His insistence on defending her dad was like salt in her wounds, stinging at the edges and making her wish she'd never agreed to this.

"It doesn't make it any easier to pack everything up and go find another place to live. Several times we had to stay with my grandparents while Dad tried to find another congregation. We'd drive to these different towns and he'd preach, there'd be a potluck for lunch so the church could get to know us, then we'd wait to hear back from them whether or not they thought we were a good fit."

Gray reached across the table and gave her hand a sympathetic squeeze. She hadn't told him the worst part yet.

"Most of the time, though, we moved simply because the elders would ask him to leave. Sometimes we never found out why. They'd just call him in to a meeting, and he'd come home and announce we were leaving soon."

"They never told you why?"

"We'd get some story like 'Several members have come to us with concerns that you're not a good fit for this congregation anymore.'" She shook her head. "We never found out which members said it or what their concerns were. So for the rest of our time there, it was hard to be friendly to anyone because you never knew who had stabbed you in the back."

A frown darkened his normally bright blue eyes. She picked at the last few bites of her egg roll, strewing cabbage across her plate. She'd never really told anyone this, not even talked about it with her family.

FRIDAY GRAY STUCK his head in the office and gave her a sad look. "Just found out I'm going to be in a meeting all afternoon. Can I take a rain check on our lunch?"

She swallowed her disappointment. As much as she'd dreaded telling him about high school, she'd come to love getting to eat lunch with him each day this week. No one had ever listened the way he did. "It's fine. Maybe next week."

Friday ended with no other sign of Gray. She grabbed her bag and headed out. Every scenario they'd run that week on the software had gone well except for three, and those were easy fixes. They'd all agreed things were going well enough they could rest this weekend and be refreshed to face the rollout week. She curled up in her yoga pants with her favorite old movies and tried to relax. Gray texted her another invitation to join him for church services, and she declined once more.

The actors danced their way across her screen, the woman's skirts flying in the right direction, every move perfectly synchronized. The whole cast knew all the words to all the songs in the movies, and no one ever doubted there would be some sort of happy ending. She hugged a pillow to her chest and sighed. Her life was just about as far as possible from being a musical.

13

With the impending rollout happening the next week, Adrian and Gray didn't get much time together to talk about anything but work. She did some last-minute visits to each office to make sure any questions were answered. Driving all over West Tennessee ensured she didn't even get to see Gray much for the first three days of the week. Thursday was D-day. She got to the office early and pulled everything up to see how it was working.

"It looks good, right?" Gray was suddenly right behind her, his face inches from hers as he peered over her shoulder.

She jumped and pressed her hand to her heart, now racing from being startled ... and possibly just the nearness of him.

"Sorry. Didn't mean to make you jump."

"It's okay. I'd grown used to the quiet and was so focused I didn't hear you come in." She pointed to her screen. "Some of the schedules didn't go over at midnight, so I'm trying to figure out what's keeping it from happening."

"Oh, wow. Yeah. We need to get that done ASAP." He pulled his chair up so he could sit beside her instead of hovering over her shoulder. "Can you tell if those clients have all of their information entered?"

"That's what I was about to check."

The rest of the morning flew by as she and Gray worked side-by-side to get all the schedules over so the healthcare providers could get paid for clocking in and out. When she finally had everything in the right place and lining up the way it was supposed to, she did a little happy dance. Gray laughed so hard he almost fell out of his chair.

"I've got to report to the managers how things are going. That will determine who works how many hours this weekend. As of this point, since you've been through this multiple times now, what do you think? Are we looking good?" Gray stood and stretched his fingers.

She leaned back to see him. "As of this moment, yes. Now if we have schedule issues again in the morning, at least one of us needs to be here every morning until we get it to automatically do what it's supposed to."

"Have you had this issue in the past?"

"We've had similar problems at other places." She glanced at her computer screen as an email notification popped up. "Most of the time we can get it squared away within the first day or two. Since this is the first time our software has had to work with your telephony provider so your people can call in and out, we weren't sure what this morning would be like. Really it wasn't as bad as a few places I've done this. We got it sorted out within four hours."

"So what should I tell the higher ups?" He leaned against the door frame.

"That I'll know more tomorrow morning but, as of this moment, things are going well." She glanced over her shoulder at him. "That's all I can promise. I know they want to be able to tell people whether they're getting any time off this weekend or not, but I honestly don't know what else might happen today or tonight. This is the part where we're just putting out fires as they appear."

Gray gave a nod. "Okay. That's what I'll pass on."

No other problems popped up the rest of the afternoon, and everything ran smoothly Friday morning. She gave Gray permission to let the managers know that things were progressing well. Brad was pleased to hear it, too, though his voice still sounded a bit strained, like there were other problems he was more worried about. He wouldn't tell her anything when she asked if he was okay, though, so she put it out of her mind.

"Looks like we might get to see fireworks after all." Late Friday afternoon, Gray stretched his legs out. They were so long in their little office area, they ended up on either side of her chair.

"If you want to go see fireworks, you should go see fireworks." Adrian deleted a few emails and closed her screen.

"Do you not like fireworks? How un-American!" His eyes twinkled with mischief.

"More like I don't want to go sit in the heat and get eaten alive by mosquitoes." She stacked some papers neatly on the corner of her desk and picked up some paperclips scattered about.

"What if I offer to provide bug repellent?"

"Are you asking me to go see fireworks with you?"

"Would you like to?" He leaned forward with his elbows on his knees. "I mean, even if we get called in to fix a problem this weekend, we'd still be done before it was dark enough for fireworks. And they have a really neat show over the river. Live music, funnel cakes, very American."

A wide grin stretched her mouth. "Okay, Gray. I'll go see fireworks with you."

ADRIAN OPENED her hotel door and held up her finger to Gray Sunday evening. "Yes. That's right. Now click on the date. Uh huh."

Gray walked around the suite while she finished with the

phone call. She motioned to the couch to indicate he could sit, but he shook his head. He wandered over and ran his finger along the titles of the DVDs stacked by the television.

"Yes. Okay. Just hit *save,* and you should see it change. Does it look right now?" She grabbed her keys and purse. "Great. Okay. Call back if you need anything else. Okay. Bye."

Gray looked up.

Adrian held up her phone. "One of the office employees was trying to remember how to change a schedule. She had it all except for the date. You'd think that would be the easiest part to remember."

"It's amazing what you can forget in a crunch."

"True. You ready?"

"All set. I have the bug repellent in the car." He walked with her down to the elevator, his hand on the small of her back. "So elevators like this don't bother you? I mean, you're on the third floor."

"I can't see how high up we are in this one. And I choose not to look out the windows of my room much."

He steered her to his car in the parking lot and opened the door for her. The sun was still up, but it crept lower on the horizon as they drove west. She flipped the visor down. It was a sticky ninety-eight degrees that felt like one hundred and eight with the humidity. Summertime in the South.

"A lot of people come downtown for this event, as well as several others, so we'll probably have to park and walk to the river." Gray maneuvered through the interstate traffic.

"That's fine." She reached over and repositioned the air conditioner vents. "I better soak up this cool air while I can."

"It did turn out hot today. We could've gone to the Redbirds game, I guess. I forgot about that."

"Redbirds?"

"The local triple-A baseball team." He waved over to his right. "The stadium is just down there. It's pretty nice. And they do fireworks after the game."

"This will probably be more fun."

They stepped out into the heat. Even in the shade of the parking garage, the perspiration was almost immediate. Was she miserable? The last thing he wanted to do was make her uncomfortable. He kept his hand on her back as they joined the throngs of people all headed toward the river.

The sun had less than half an hour of light left, and the sky showed off with streaks of red, purple, and orange, as if to prove it could be just as pretty as the light show coming later. They passed several food trucks, all wafting fabulous aromas of fried delicacies and sugar. A local group sang their hearts out on a stage to the right of them, and several people in the crowd danced.

"Do you want to go down closer to the river?" He pointed through the masses toward the water.

"It's up to you. I figure we'll have a pretty good view from any spot down here, right?" The sky gave her no indication of where the rockets would go off.

"Yeah. But it's prettier when you can see it reflected in the water too. Come on." He gently took her arm and steered her through the horde.

There were even more people down near the river, picnic blankets and lawn chairs staking territory. Children ran around with glow sticks and cotton candy. Couples strolled along the sidewalk, holding hands. Gray found a spot between two other families and confirmed it wasn't taken before pulling an old quilt out of the backpack he was carrying.

"Voila!" He gestured toward their spot with a flourish.

"Very nice." She sank to the ground and took in the view. A few boats were out on the water, but not many. Birds soared and dove overhead, enjoying a late-night feast of the bugs swarming the area. The sunlight and sky reflected off the Pyramid up the river.

"How's your dad?" Gray settled next to her, his arm on the quilt behind her.

"He's good. Danny sends me updates every day. He's home and worrying mom. She's not used to having him underfoot so much. I have no idea what they'll do if he ever retires." She swatted at a mosquito.

Gray laughed. "I'm glad he's doing better. He seemed in pretty good spirits when we were there a couple weeks ago. It's crazy that it's been so long now. This summer is going by too fast."

"I still can't believe you guys came all that way." She glanced over at him. "You're insane."

"It's what Christians do. They try to be there for each other in times of need."

ADRIAN SHOOK HER HEAD. "Not all of them."

"Our lunches sort of got interrupted, and we never finished your story." Gray reached over and brushed a stray hair from her face. "Want to tell me some more?"

Who knew the merest brush of his fingers against her skin could elicit such a strong tremor in her tummy? Or was that the fear of finishing what she'd started? She released a breath and stared out over the river toward Arkansas. Her supposed home state.

"Where were we? Middle school?"

"And you didn't fit in because your dad was your Sunday school teacher."

She gave a semi-grin. "Or something like that. Yeah. So we moved again my sixth-grade year. Talk about not fitting in. That group decided if you hadn't lived in that town your whole life, you couldn't be in the 'in' crowd. I tried to blow it off and pretend like it didn't bother me, but it hurt."

She wouldn't tell him everything. Though memories did laps through her head—the time the jerk snuck a condom into her locker in ninth grade to humiliate her because she was the 'good girl who didn't believe in sex before marriage.' The rude names people called her to her face, the way others quit talking whenever she joined them as if she wasn't good enough to join their discussion. No. Some things still hurt too much to bring to light in the present.

"Even the church kids?" He leaned forward with his knees up in front of him.

"Especially the church kids. The other kids at school were actually friendlier most of the time."

"Kids are so mean." His voice made her want to ask him about his childhood. "So how long were you at this place?"

"Six years. It's the longest I've lived anywhere. By the end of it, I was actually finding a niche. I had several friends I thought were close. I ordered my senior ring—you know you do that junior year instead of senior, so you can wear it longer. Everything was going great. Then right before Easter, Dad got called in to one of those elder meetings. He and Mom gathered us, and we did pizza in the living room. That should have clued me in. We never ate in the living room."

"Really?" He looked over at her.

"Really." She rolled her eyes. "My mom was a huge stickler for having the family around the dinner table every night she could. Eating in the living room was a rare treat. We were going to watch a movie together as a family, but between dinner and the movie, he told us we'd have to move over the summer. I wanted to die. Having to start over again your senior year of high school ..."

"That's rough."

She nodded. "I think that was a huge turning point for me. I mean, it'd taken me almost all six years to find a place to fit, to find friends, to really start feeling like it could be home. Then *wham*! Time to move again."

"Why did you have to move that time?" His hand rested on top of hers.

She didn't pull away. "That was one of the times we never

really found out why. Someone got upset about something, and the elders evidently decided it was serious enough to ask Dad to step down. He was never told what the reason was or who the upset people were. It truly felt like the church had stabbed us in the back."

A rocket whistled to their right, and they turned to see the explosion of red sparkles. It was almost completely dark now. She hadn't even realized the sun had gone down. Gray pulled her closer to him, and she didn't complain despite the heat.

"I'm sorry you had to go through that." He had to speak right in her ear to be heard over the fireworks. "But you have to remember that the church is made up of people. They're not perfect, and they make mistakes. You can't blame God for the decisions people made."

She turned to look at him, wanting to argue. "You don't understand."

"No. I don't understand exactly what you went through. But it sounds like most of your hurt came from people, not God." His face was so close to hers, his breath on her cheek. He reached up to wipe a tear from her face she hadn't even realized was there.

Before she knew what was happening, the hand that had caressed her cheek so gently to wipe away her sadness pulled her just a little closer, and his lips touched hers. Her eyes fluttered closed, her breath caught in her throat. The kiss was only a few seconds, but time might as well have stopped.

She jumped as a particularly loud firecracker exploded overhead. His eyes held hers for a moment longer before they mutually looked to the sky. Had that just happened? Her racing pulse told her something had moved her, and she knew it wasn't the patriotic music playing in the background.

They watched the rest of the show in silence, standing for the end with everyone else, cheering as the last round of fireworks made the sky almost as bright as day for a few splendored seconds. It was almost deafeningly quiet when the bursts ended. She rubbed her bare arms, not really cold but lonely for the heat his arms had provided.

"It will be crazy to get out of here right away. Do you want to join the mass exodus or wait around a bit longer?" Gray motioned toward everyone walking around them.

"Tomorrow is a workday." She was slightly amazed her voice had come out normal.

"Every day seems to be a workday for you."

She could see the tease in his grin, even in the dim light of the streetlights. "That's me. All work and no play."

"I'm working on that." He shook the quilt out to brush off any stray blades of grass.

She wasn't sure what to reply to that. Did she want him working on her? Did she want him to stop? Did she wish he would kiss her again? Did she have a clue what was going on?

The only answer she could come up with for any of those questions was to the last one, and it was a resounding *no*.

14

Adrian took a sip of coffee and pretended her lips weren't still remembering the kiss from the night before. It was past time to get out the door and start toward the office, but she lingered a moment longer, trying to sort through the chaos in her mind before facing Gray again. They hadn't said much on the way back last night, and he hadn't tried to kiss her again when he dropped her off.

With a shake of her head, she poured the last few drops down the sink. She couldn't be late for work even if she wasn't fully ready to face her coworker again. Grabbing her bag, she strode out to tackle the day.

"Good morning!" Gray smiled as she came in.

Was that expression any friendlier than normal? She couldn't tell. And didn't want to stare any longer than normal lest he realize she was still dwelling on last night.

"Morning." She set up her laptop and listened to it hum as it booted up. A few clicks and she had her email pulled up.

"Want to do lunch today?" Gray glanced at her over his shoulder.

"Can't. I just stopped by here first to refill my coffee and check emails really fast, make sure nothing is going wrong around here, before I hit the road. Brad wants me to swing by the other offices over the next few days to answer any questions and show a few employees some things they've done incorrectly."

She pointed to the email on her screen. "I need to visit the closer ones today and tomorrow: Millington, Bartlett, Collierville. Then Dyersburg and Jackson will be Wednesday and Thursday."

"That's a lot of driving. Especially since you just went to those places last week."

"Yeah, but I want to make sure all of your employees know exactly what to do. And we do need to nip a few things in the bud on doing things wrong." She shrugged. "It's not so bad being on the road, really. It's a nice break from being stuck in a dungeon all day."

"Can't argue with you there." He scooted back a bit as she closed her laptop and placed it back in her bag. "Be careful."

"Of course." She slung the strap over her shoulder.

"Adrian, really." Gray grabbed her hand before she could leave. "Please be careful."

His fingers holding hers captured her attention for a full minute. "I'm always careful, Gray. I'm going to get more coffee and head out. I'm sure I'll be in and out throughout the week. And then we get to help tackle payroll for the first time since switching to this software. Yay."

"Payroll." He smirked. "There's something to look forward to."

"See ya later." She pulled away and left their office space.

Even though she usually liked visiting all the offices of the company she worked with since it gave her some variety and quiet time in the car, today she was loath to leave the basement despite what she'd told Gray. She could still feel the pressure of his fingers on hers as she fixed her coffee. Why was she even dwelling on this? A relationship between them had no chance. St. Louis and Memphis weren't exactly right next to each other.

Brad called her a little later, and she opened the call on her speakers. "Hey, Boss."

"Good morning, Adrian. You got my email?"

"I'm on my way to Millington as we speak." She changed lanes to pass a slower car. "I'll be up there this morning, do Bartlett on the way back in. Then tomorrow, I'll head down to Collierville and hit Cordova on the way back. Wednesday and Thursday will be Dyersburg and Jackson."

"Sounds good. And they're starting payroll Friday, right?" She could hear his papers flipping in the background.

"They'll actually start working on things Wednesday. We have to have it all cleaned up and ready to go by the end of Monday so they can get checks printed and sent out before the fifteenth." Her GPS told her to turn right at the next light, and she hit her turn signal.

"Should you try to do the offices farther out today and tomorrow instead so that you can be closer while they're working on payroll?"

"They have you guys and Gray." She tapped her steering wheel as she talked. "And really what they're doing is verifying time worked. I can't help much with that. They'll need me more when they export it all to our software and then try to send it from there to their program to cut checks. I have a feeling that's where any real problems will pop up."

"You're the expert."

"Ha. I'm not sure about expert, but thanks. It's nice to have job security." She stopped at a red light.

Quiet echoed for a long moment on his end. "Okay. Well, be safe, and call if you need anything. I'll be in touch."

She wondered about the distraction in his voice but put it from her mind as she got closer to the office. This week and next would be busy, just the kind of weeks she liked. Having time to think was overrated.

HE HADN'T MEANT to kiss her. Not really.

The moment had been perfect though. And he had no regrets. If only he could tell whether or not she was of the same mind. That's why he'd wanted to do lunch Monday.

Instead for the last few days he'd had his office back to himself. And he hated it. It no longer smelled like flowers. No chance of bumping into anyone ... accidentally or on purpose. And no humming.

Truly a dungeon.

"If you're moping this badly now, what are you going to be like when she leaves?"

Great. Now he was talking to himself.

"Gray."

He jumped. "What?"

Miranda stood in his doorway. "What was the title of that movie you mentioned in the trivia game a few weeks ago?"

"You're going to have to be more specific than that." He held up a finger. "Or here. I can print out the list again, and you can skim it to find the one you're looking for."

"Great. Thanks." She grabbed the paper off the printer and was gone as quickly as she'd appeared.

Had she heard him asking himself about Adrian? Too late now.

Adrian wouldn't have to ask what the movie was. He was pretty sure she'd known every single one he quizzed about, not that she'd answered them all. If he were to guess, he'd say she probably didn't even want to answer the ones she had but couldn't stand the thought of no one else guessing either.

What was the movie pictured on her computer homepage? He'd seen the DVD case at her hotel the other night but couldn't think of the title now. Too bad he didn't have it on a list too. He'd recognized one of the stars ... Judy Garland.

"Judy ..." He quickly typed her name in the search and skimmed through all the films listed. "There. *Meet Me in St.*

Louis." He chuckled to himself. "Appropriate. It's where she lives."

As he researched it more, several ads appeared on the edge of his screen, including one he found he couldn't ignore. What were the dates? *Please let the dates work out.*

It was a frivolous prayer but one he couldn't avoid sending up. This was too good to be true. Tomorrow through the weekend. If they went tomorrow, it would be before payroll chaos really started and there'd be less risk of having to leave early.

Would she agree?

God, please, let her agree. And please help me remember that even though she was once a Christian, she doesn't consider herself one now. If You can use me to help her see that all people who believe in You aren't like the ones from her past, I'd love it. If not, please let her see it another way. God, I long for her to return to You more than I long for anything to work out between the two of us.

But if you could make them both happen, even better. Please?

"I HAVE A SURPRISE FOR YOU." Gray grinned at her as she walked into the office late Thursday afternoon.

"Oh? Payroll is done, and everything went perfectly?" Adrian was in work mode and couldn't think of any other possibilities.

"No. It's actually something happening later this evening." He leaned back in his seat. "Will you trust me enough to come?"

A huge part of her wanted to say, 'No.' The other part was screaming, 'YES!' As busy as she'd been this week, driving allowed her much too much time to think—and that had left her missing Gray, despite telling her heart nothing could come of it. She hesitated, thinking about possible options for a surprise.

"I promise it's something you'll absolutely love. I know it without a doubt." He crossed his chest with his finger.

It was a little unnerving to think he might know her so well in such a short time that he could make such a promise. Also flattering. She'd never had a guy try to figure her out, to want to surprise her, to be so tempting.

"Please?" He leaned forward and clasped his hands in front of him in playful pleading.

She couldn't fight the smile trying to escape. "Will you tell me what it is if I agree to go?"

"Nope. You'll just have to wait and see."

"Is it something dressy?" She set her laptop up to try and regain her focus on what she was supposed to be doing.

"No. Casual." He tapped a pen against his desk. "I'll pick you up a little after seven. It starts around 8:30 ... if you agree to go."

She trusted him. It almost petrified her how much she trusted him. She made him wait a few more seconds, though, just to keep him on his toes.

"Okay."

He placed his hand on her shoulder. "Thanks for trusting me."

"Should I eat beforehand, or does it include dinner?"

"Maybe dessert."

"Oh good, you're here." Diane from Accounting stuck her head in the door of their office before Adrian could say anything else to Gray. "We may have a problem."

It was four o'clock. She mentally crossed her fingers that this issue wouldn't take more than an hour. Now that she'd let herself be talked into this date, she didn't want to miss it. Date? That word made it a bit scarier. And yet, she couldn't deny wanting it either.

The problem turned out to be someone clicking the wrong button. Once Adrian showed them again which boxes to select to get their reports, the "crisis" was averted. Gray wasn't in their office as she gathered her things to leave. She swallowed her disappointment by reminding herself he would pick her up in just a few hours.

Back at the hotel, she pulled on her favorite jeans and a

blouse with flutter sleeves. A hasty peek in the mirror revealed that her makeup and hair were still okay. After slipping into some sandals, she sat down to finish checking the email she hadn't had time for earlier that afternoon—anything to try and keep from wondering what the surprise would be. Halfheartedly she picked at a frozen dinner she microwaved, careful not to drip any sauce.

He knocked on her door at seven-fifteen, and she made herself wait a second so he wouldn't think she'd been standing right beside it, waiting.

"Ready to go?"

She nodded and grabbed her purse. "Ready as I'll ever be to go I have no idea where."

"You don't like surprises?" He looked nice in a pair of jeans and a white-striped polo shirt.

"They're not always my favorite." She shrugged. "I've had some lousy ones in the past."

"This one isn't going to be lousy." He opened the car door for her and let her slide in. "I promise."

This evening he drove north instead of west. She recognized some of the area and watched the brick storefronts of Germantown as they drove by. She caught herself humming with the song on the radio before she realized it was a hymn. Did he always play worship songs in his car? She couldn't remember what played the last few times she'd ridden with him.

"Here we are." He pulled into a drive and gestured to a big white screen.

"A drive-in theater."

"Yes." He grinned, obviously proud of himself. "I know you like movies. What do you think?"

"It's great, Gray. I didn't even pay attention to what you were telling the ticket lady as we came in because I was so busy looking around. What's showing?" She peered over her shoulder to attempt to see the sign.

He fiddled with the radio dial until he was tuned to the

frequency the theater used for their sound. "I think it's one of your favorites."

"One of my favorites?" She leaned back in her seat and got comfortable.

"I was snooping the titles of your movies the other day when I came to pick you up. And I noticed the picture on your computer background."

Her heart skipped a beat. "*Meet Me in St. Louis?*"

He nodded as the sound came on the radio. "I was researching it online to find out more about it and discovered they were doing this special showing." He rolled the windows down to let a breeze come through. The sun was setting, and the screen would soon light up.

"It is one of my favorites." She looked around, glanced at Gray, shook her head, then studied her hands. "Has been for a long time. It's the movie we watched the night Dad announced we were leaving again my junior year."

"Oh, wow. You said you watched a movie that night but didn't mention what it was. I would think you'd hate a movie associated with that memory."

She tilted her head as she thought about it. "I loved the story of it, though. I really hoped it would happen to us. Have you seen it?"

"Not yet."

"The family finds out they have to move because of the father's job. They're all upset and saying their goodbyes and packing things. Then—spoiler alert—Christmas night, the father sees how miserable everyone is, and he decides they won't move after all. They get to stay in St. Louis."

He rested his hand on hers. "Is that why you wanted to live in St. Louis?"

"Wow." She met his gaze. "Huh. I guess maybe it is. I never even considered why I wanted to live there. Just that it held this feeling of somewhere I wouldn't have to leave again. I've been uprooted so many times, and I guess I somehow thought if I found a place like in my favorite movie, maybe I could stay."

"I don't think I've ever actually seen someone make a breakthrough before." He laughed. "It was sort of like a light bulb went on in your eyes just now."

"It's just so neat to be able to put my finger on something I've never really been able to answer before. Remember when you asked me several weeks ago why I wanted to live there? Now we both know."

He reached around his seat and pulled a cooler from the back. "I almost forgot."

She leaned over to see inside as he opened it. He pulled out a carton of ice cream and handed it to her. The music on the radio changed as he handed her a bowl and spoon and pulled out chocolate sauce and whipped cream. Giggles bubbled up inside her. This was possibly the most perfect date she could've imagined.

Just a hint of pink and purple lingered in the sky as the screen flickered to life. A thrill ran through her as the opening credits flashed so large in front of her. Gray squirted whipped cream on top of her sundae and held out the can with a quirked brow. "Want some in your mouth?"

The giggle escaped. "No, but thanks. This is perfect."

PERFECT. She said it was perfect. And even better, they'd both learned something else about her too. Although he'd prefer not to have a console between them. When did they quit making cars where a couple could snuggle during a drive-in movie?

She hummed along as Judy Garland sang about loving the boy next door.

Gray turned his head and grinned. "You can sing out loud, ya know? We're not in a real theater where you have to be quiet."

"Sorry." She ducked her head. "I've warned you about my humming tendency."

"I love that you hum all the time. It means you have music in your soul. You shouldn't apologize for that." He ran a finger down the side of her face.

Her skin was softer than he'd imagined. He forced himself to focus on the film once more and sang along with "The Trolley Song," one of the tunes they'd sung at the banquet over a month before. She gave in and joined him for that one and then quietly sang along with all the movie's other songs.

A soft sigh escaped her lips as the closing scene wrapped up. He agreed. The story left a sense of peace and happiness inside. She looked over at Gray and smiled.

"Thank you."

"You're welcome." He squeezed her hand. "That was fun. I can see why you like it. Of course, now I'll probably have that Christmas song stuck in my head and drive myself crazy since it's only July."

She laughed. "Yeah. That's probably the only downside to watching that movie when it's not December."

"That scene near the end was hilarious though. Where he bursts in and declares his love for the older sister." He rolled up the windows and followed the other cars out of the parking lot.

"I love that scene. I can be in the worst mood and put that movie in, and that part makes me laugh every time."

"What would you do if someone just randomly came in and pointed at you and exclaimed, 'I love you'?" He glanced over at her before he turned onto the road.

"It's not going to happen. I mean, I think it would be really fun. But it's not going to happen." She stared out the window as they wound their way back toward her hotel.

"It might. It's not like you're unlovable."

She shot him a skeptical look. "I guess my nephews love me."

"Have you ever given anyone else a chance to love you?" Something told him he'd hit the nail on the head.

"What's that supposed to mean?" She tucked one of her legs under her and leaned toward the door.

"I mean you have this habit of trying to keep everyone at arm's length or farther. I get that you got hurt growing up when you let people get closer, but that doesn't mean it's going to happen every time. What if someone wanted to get closer?" He glanced her way as they pulled up to a red light.

What about me?

ADRIAN PICKED an excuse out of the list she kept for when her sister asked personal questions. "My life isn't exactly copacetic for a relationship. I'm never in St. Louis for more than a few weeks, it seems. And then I'm spending a month here, three months there. That doesn't exactly scream, 'Try to build something lasting with me!'"

"But what if someone wanted to anyway?"

What could she say? Was he talking about himself? Admittedly she'd been enjoying their time together. She looked forward to seeing him and hearing his way-too-cheerful 'good morning' each day. Who knew how many times she'd relived their kiss?

He pulled into the parking lot of her hotel and turned the car off. "Adrian, you are an amazing woman. You've intrigued me from the first time I saw you on my computer screen. Would you consider giving a relationship with me a chance?"

Her heart skipped a beat. She wanted to shout, 'Yes!' But terror churned in her stomach, turning her sundae into a milkshake. Did he realize what he was asking?

"I'll only be here a few more weeks at most. Then I'm off to St. Louis and out to another company to train them. That's my job. I can't just stay here."

"Okay." He stared without blinking.

"Gray, I live in St. Louis."

"I know that."

"You live in Memphis." She pointed out the window.

"I know that, too."

"You realize they're not exactly right next to each other, right?" She waved her hands in the air.

"Yes, Adrian. I realize they're not next to each other." He leaned forward and caught her hands in his. "But I also realize God can work things out if we want them to work."

She pulled her hands out of his. "But I don't know that. I know you have faith in Him, but mine is still wavering. And I know you're not really okay with that. You need to find some good Christian girl who comes with a perfect history to match yours. Someone who can share your faith without having all these doubts and anger and hurt."

"Adrian—"

"I'm sorry, Gray." She got out of the car before he could say anything else. Back inside her hotel room, she wrapped her arms around herself and slid to the floor. Tears streamed down her face as she cried for what might have been.

PERFECTION GONE, just like that. He beat his fist against the steering wheel. She thought his past was spotless.

Ha!

Hadn't he thought the other day that he'd tell her his history once she got done with hers? And then work had taken over, and they hadn't found time. And now here he sat, a fool for not having acted before now. Too late.

Would she even talk to him again? Now that she knew he wanted to be more than simply coworkers? She'd have to at least talk about work things.

"Not enough."

A glance at the windows in the building did him no good in

determining which was hers. Was she as upset as he was? The way she'd run, she had to have been.

He cranked the engine too hard and then grimaced as it protested. No point in hurting his car over this. That would only make matters worse. Time to go home and do some more praying. Maybe he'd misread the direction God was trying to point him.

His phone rang as he stepped through his front door. "Mom."

"You were on my heart. Everything okay?"

"No." He glanced at the clock. "It's late. Why are you still up?"

"I told you that already. You know I can't sleep when God is telling me to pray and help." Her voice was scolding but also worried.

He dropped his keys into the dish by the door and flopped into his favorite chair. "You're right. I'm not okay."

"What's wrong? Are you sick?"

"No." He shook his head. "Not physically anyway."

"What does that mean?"

He huffed out a sigh. "Maybe I'm lovesick."

"Grayson." The hope in her voice was heartbreaking.

"Don't start planning grandbabies yet. She's not interested in a relationship."

"Why not?"

"It's a long story." He rubbed his temple.

"I'm not sleeping anyway. Might as well tell me. That way, I can be more specific with my prayers."

He chuckled. "Better get Dad on here too, so I don't have to tell it twice."

His parents listened as he filled them in on his unexplainable attraction from the first moment he'd seen Adrian, to getting to know her through the lunches, to the problem she had with God, and then on to the disaster of a date tonight.

Through it all, Mom clucked her sympathies and Dad hummed

every now and then to assure he was listening. From the first moment he'd met his parents, they'd supported him through everything. If he could trust anyone's judgment on this, it was theirs.

Why hadn't he gone to them before now?

"Well?" Gray prompted when he was done. "Am I a complete nincompoop?"

"Of course not!" Mom protested.

"Though maybe a bit hasty." Dad chimed in.

Gray agreed more with Dad. "I need prayers. The next few days at work will be crazy as we try to get payroll ready to go in the midst of switching to this new software. I'll have to focus on business and not on Adrian. And the same for her. I can't be a distraction."

"We'll be praying," Dad said. "For both of you."

"Thanks."

"We always pray for you, Gray. But now we have a name to pray when we pray for your future spouse too." Mom's voice was confident. Much more confident than Gray was.

"Mom ..."

"Just let her pray, Gray. If God wants it to happen, He'll show you how to work it out." Dad chuckled.

The talk with his parents calmed him down enough to settle for the night. He still had a bit of praying to do of his own. But now, he had a feeling he'd have a better chance of getting some sleep before he had to face Adrian once more.

God, grant her some rest too. And some peace.

15

Adrian awoke to an early-morning thunderstorm. Lightning illuminated her room before another clap of thunder shook the earth. She climbed out of bed and pulled the curtains back enough to see rain coming down in sheets.

The sky was still mostly dark with night, and the clouds obscured any bit of sun that might have come up. She closed the drapes again and padded to the kitchen to start her coffee maker. Maybe a cup of java and a shower would make this day look better, although she doubted it.

She wiped the steam from the mirror in the bathroom after her shower and grimaced at her reflection. It was after eleven when Gray had dropped her off and then much later when she gave up and went to bed. She finally fell asleep in the early hours of the morning.

With the rain pouring down outside, her hair was fit for nothing better than a ponytail. She pulled on a peasant-style top with her capris. It was a Friday, but it was also time to help with the first payroll. She dreaded going to work this morning for multiple reasons.

"I'm a professional. I can do this."

While she sipped her creamy coffee, she checked her email.

The hot liquid felt good going down her throat and into her belly. Her head cleared some as the caffeine kicked in, and she sharpened her resolve to be a professional more than anything else. The accounting department was relying on her today, and she couldn't let last night hamper her ability to give them her best.

With the wind blowing outside, an umbrella would be useless. She grabbed a jacket with a hood, threw it on over her bag, too, then ducked out into the deluge and dashed to the car. Her pants were mostly soaked by the time she got the door unlocked and slid into the driver's seat. She kicked the heater on. It might be July, but the wet was chilly and left her shivering.

Drivers in Memphis were normally bad, but on days like this one, it was as if they lost all ability to drive at all. She clenched the steering wheel as she maneuvered the streets between her hotel and the office.

There were no parking spots left without a deep puddle, so she gave up and braced herself to have wet feet. She pulled her hood back up and hurried through the lot and into the office. If her nails hadn't been painted bright red, her toes would've been completely blue.

She tried to shake off as much water as she could in the entryway, but evidence of other wet feet trailed down the carpeted hallway, so she followed suit. Pulling her jacket off as she walked to the stairs, she folded it in on itself so that it would drip as little as possible. The frigid air of the basement was unbearable on her damp skin.

Outside of Gray's office, she paused and took a deep breath. *I am a professional. He is a coworker. I'm only here another couple weeks at the most. I can do this.*

She straightened her shoulders and held her head high as she walked in. He wasn't even there. Her backbone relaxed, and she pulled her laptop out of the bag and set it up to get her workday started.

A particularly loud clap of thunder shook the building, and

the lights flickered and went out. The darkness was thick around her. Only her computer screen provided a glow in the small room. She turned around and looked out toward the hall, but it was pitch black too. Carefully, she stood and walked toward where the door was, feeling her way to make sure she didn't bump into the desk. As she reached the doorway, she smacked into a body instead.

"Adrian?" Gray's hands gripped her upper arms.

She took a step back. "Yes. Don't we have a generator or something?"

"Yeah. One of the maintenance guys is cranking it up now." His hands squeezed her biceps. "You're wet."

"It's raining, in case you hadn't noticed."

"The reason I keep an extra set of clothes here."

She shook the image of him changing clothes out of her head. Not appropriate for maintaining any kind of business relationship.

"Can I get around you for a second?"

"Oh, yeah. Sorry." She scooted toward the wall but still felt his body brush against hers as he eased around to his desk.

"I'll need to go around and make sure everyone's computer boots back up correctly once the generator kicks in. Do you need anything before I go?"

She shook her head before remembering he couldn't see her. "No. I'm okay. Once the lights come back on, I'll go check with accounting and see how things are looking."

"Okay. You've got my cell number so just give me a holler if anything comes up." He rummaged around somewhere in the dark, but she couldn't discern what was making the sounds. "I think I have a jacket here somewhere. Feel free to look when the lights are back."

She felt him squeeze past her again, his cologne lingering in the air.

"Sure." She swallowed her sadness. *He's a professional too. Just doing his job. He doesn't have time to talk about last night.* She found her way back to her chair and sat in front of her laptop without seeing it. *This is what I wanted. Get it together.*

The lights came back on with a flash and hum. Gray's computer beeped behind her as it started up. Thunder rolled again, but not as strong, as if it might be a little farther out.

"Adrian?" Diane stuck her head in the office. "Something tells me this day won't go as well as we had hoped."

Adrian followed Diane back to Accounting and scanned the first reports pulled for payroll. Nothing looked right. She took a breath, nodded, and prepared herself to find the problem and help this company get its payroll done in time. This was why she was here—not to have her heart hurt by a handsome man.

Though she wished she'd had time to find that jacket.

IT WAS JUST AS WELL Gray hadn't been able to stay in that dark space with Adrian. When he'd felt her trembling under his hands, all he'd wanted to do was wrap her up in his arms. Not exactly conducive to keeping things professional.

The more he'd thought and prayed about the situation last night, the more he'd decided maybe he'd moved too fast. If he'd listened to his brain at the beginning of all this, when he was determined to stay away because she wasn't a Christian, maybe things wouldn't be so awkward now. Instead, he'd pushed all that aside and gone all in.

Well, in as deep as a guy could be without revealing his own past, that is.

"Gray, I need you!" Michael called from the server room.

"On my way."

The way this day was starting, at least he shouldn't have much time to think. Or any way to try and convince Adrian to give him another chance. Hopefully, he'd find a moment to pray here and there, at least. He'd need to make sure of that.

Once the servers were back up, as well as all the computers

and phones, he checked messages once more. Several panicked notes were on his screen, all having to do with payroll. Great. So much for no problems.

He spun his chair to head toward Accounting and noticed the edge of the jacket he'd told Adrian to look for. She might not welcome a relationship, but maybe she'd welcome the warmth? Grabbing it, he walked upstairs to face the chaos.

Adrian barely had time to give him a smile of thanks when he draped the coat over her shoulders. She worked between three different computers at once, laptop balanced on her lap. He had no idea how she kept up with which program was open on which monitor, but he was impressed. Once more, this woman left him amazed at her fortitude and ability to multitask.

"Can you grab that off the printer, please?" Diane waved his direction.

Grateful for something to do, he dashed into the hallway to find what she'd requested.

"Thanks." Diane skimmed numbers, shaking her head. "No. We're still not pulling everything. This is maybe half our workers."

"Okay." Adrian scratched her head with the pencil in her hand before shoving it into her ponytail for later. "Let's see. We've checked here and made sure all the boxes were clicked. Oh, wait. Here's a suggestion from Brad. Let's see."

"Give me something to do." Gray sat down at another computer nearby.

"Here." Adrian forwarded him a couple of options Brad had sent. "See if you can get those to work while I try these."

"You got it." He forced his focus to the numbers and commands in front of him, making sure he didn't miss any steps. Sending up a prayer for help, he entered the first sequence, but it didn't seem to pull any more than they already had. Good thing he'd had a big breakfast this morning. Something told him he wasn't getting lunch.

A rumble of thunder seemed to confirm it. When he'd

wanted to spend more time with Adrian, this wasn't exactly what he had in mind. He was actually jealous of the jacket hugging her shoulders right now.

AROUND NINE-THIRTY THAT EVENING, Adrian collapsed on her couch with a paper bag of French fries and a chocolate shake. It had taken five or six people working constantly until an hour ago to get the payroll reports looking correct. She propped her feet up on the coffee table and dipped a fry in the chocolate before stuffing it in her mouth. Her phone dinged.

Hey sis. You okay? Haven't heard from you in the last few days.

She used one hand to text back while she continued to eat with the other.

Just busy.

Busy with work or busy with Gray?

Adrian resisted the urge to chuck her phone across the room.

Work. Don't want to talk about Gray.

Instead of getting another text, her phone rang.

"I just got back to my hotel and am eating. Do you really want to try and talk to me with food in my mouth?" Adrian inhaled another fry to prove her point.

"Something just told me you need to talk about Gray." Danny's voice was quiet on the other end of the line.

"I just said I didn't want to talk about him, so whatever told you I did was wrong."

"Adie, come on. This is me you're talking to. What's going on?"

Adrian took a long swig of milkshake. "What do you mean?"

"There's something wrong. I know you. We're twins. We have the twin thing going on where we can know when something isn't right with the other one. Remember when I fell on the playground in second grade and broke my arm? You knew it even though you were all the way on the other side and couldn't see me. You could just sense that something awful had happened."

Adrian rolled her eyes. "Do you really expect me to buy into that?"

"If you won't talk to me right now, I'll come over there and make you talk face to face."

"Danny, it's almost ten o'clock at night, and you're over two hours away."

"You know what I mean. I can be there by lunchtime tomorrow." Danny had her mom voice going.

"I won't talk to you about anything, now or tomorrow, so you might as well save your gas. I'm tired and about to go to bed. Today was crazy at work, and I need to sleep." Adrian threw her empty wrappers away and headed into the bedroom to find her pajamas.

"Last warning. Now or tomorrow."

"No. Stop bullying me. I love you. Goodnight." Adrian ended the call before Danny could argue any further. She didn't have the brainpower to deal with it tonight. She pulled her ponytail down and massaged the back of her head where the rubber band had been too tight.

ADRIAN WOKE up when her phone vibrated so hard it fell off the nightstand and hit the floor. She sat up and pushed hair out of her face. The sunlight sneaking in around the curtains confirmed the arrival of morning. She reached down and picked up the phone to see who had been calling—six missed calls from Danielle.

It was a little after ten o'clock—much later than she normally slept, but slumber had come hard once she finally gained dreamland. She crawled out of bed, washed her face, and started coffee before she checked her voicemails. A slight panic hit her as she realized something else might have happened to Dad.

She accessed her voicemail and hit *speaker*.

"Adie, I'm on my way to Memphis to talk to you face to face. I warned you. Call me back to let me know where to meet you."

"Seriously, Adrian, are you not up yet? I'm about an hour out. Call me back."

"Come on, Adie. I will go to every hotel in the city if I need to. This is crazy. What's going on?"

Adrian shook her head. *She's insane.*

The last three messages were very similar. "Adrian, I'm on your side of the river. Call me back and tell me where to meet you. Come on, sis. Where are you?"

Adrian took a sip of her coffee before she called her sister back. "Are you crazy?"

"Oh, good. You're up. Where do you want to meet? Or where is your hotel? I can come there."

"Danny, what if I'd had to work this morning?" Adrian padded over to her computer and woke it up to make sure there were no urgent messages she might have missed. Anything to get out of this.

"But the fact you said that tells me you're not."

Adrian barely controlled a growl. "Fine. Where are you?" Talking her sister through the winding route to the hotel, she had a bad feeling she'd regret this. "If I don't answer right away, it's because I'm in the shower."

As she toweled off her hair, there was a knock. Checking the peephole, she made sure it was her sister before she unlocked and opened the door. Danielle blew in, looking way too good for a mom of two boys who'd been up long enough to drive from Little Rock to Memphis.

One hand on her hip, Danny turned and studied Adrian. Adrian didn't stay still to let her perusal continue. Instead, she threw her towel on the table and walked back into the kitchen to reheat her coffee. Danny followed and leaned against the counter.

"You're here. See my face? I'm fine. Do you feel stupid?" Adrian took a sip of coffee and grimaced as the too-hot liquid scorched the roof of her mouth.

"No. I'm thinking I'm running late, actually. You look awful."

"You're too sweet. Want some coffee?"

When Danny shook her head, Adrian took her own and went back out in the living area to sink onto the couch.

"Seriously, Adrian." Danny flopped down beside her. "What's going on with you? You look completely different than you did over a month ago when you visited Mom and Dad. And I know you've been working like crazy, but I've never had you refuse to talk about someone who you claim is 'just a coworker' before."

"What makes you think just because you're here I'll tell you something I wouldn't tell you last night?" Adrian crisscrossed her legs in front of her.

"I'm hoping that my being here will encourage you to let out whatever is obviously upsetting you so you can sound like yourself again."

"Where are the boys today?" Adrian set her mug down on the coffee table.

"With Phil. I told him you needed me."

Adrian fixed her sister with a stare. "Just because we're twins doesn't mean you know me better than I know myself. Why couldn't I just be completely exhausted? I helped the company go through their first payroll and was at the office for almost thirteen hours yesterday. Why can't I simply not want to talk about Gray because he's just a coworker?"

"Have you heard the way you say his name?" Danielle gave

back a stare of her own. "Do you have any idea how you looked before and after he showed up when we were at the hospital with Dad? It was like he flipped a switch in you, turned a light on I hadn't seen in so long."

The desire to deny it was fierce. She sat there and gazed at the face so much like her own, the sister who'd been through everything she'd been through and yet come out of it so differently. And she knew she needed to give in to her twin and let everything out.

"I'll tell you about Gray if you answer a question for me."

Danny raised an eyebrow. "Okay. Spill."

16

A drian wished her sister would go first but knew Danny wasn't going to let up until she gave her something. How much did she want to tell? Honestly, nothing. But that was no longer an option. Time to start at the beginning and see what happened.

"Gray is ... amazing."

That wasn't what she meant to say. Danny smiled and leaned farther back into the couch as if to settle in for a good story. Adrian had a feeling Danny wouldn't like the way this one ended.

"I don't know. I mean, I first 'met' him on a video conference for work." She used her fingers to make air quotes. "We were finalizing plans for me to be here, and the first thing I noticed about him was his smile. It made my heart skip a beat. I blew it off, thinking I was just crazy. But I couldn't get him out of my mind though I'd only seen him for a few minutes over a computer screen."

"Was this before you visited Mom and Dad?" Danny propped her elbow against a pillow and leaned on her hand.

"Yes. How did you know?"

"I thought there was something you weren't telling me, remember?" She pointed at Adrian. "I was right."

"Nobody likes a know-it-all." Adrian scowled.

"Okay, okay. But I was right, for the record. Please, continue."

"You're ornery." Adrian nudged Danny with her toe but gave in and continued. "I also knew from that first meeting that he's a Christian. He told me he was praying for the success of our training sessions and transition to the new software. I figured we'd have all sorts of problems because it seems like every time I've prayed for something, God has let it turn out the opposite of how I prayed."

"You know that's not the way it works."

"No. I don't."

Danny shot her a mom look, but Adrian ignored it.

"Anyway, that first day I was here and he walked out to greet me, his smile was even more amazing in person. Then I found out we'd be sharing this tiny little office space while I work here. I wasn't thrilled, but I figured it was only for a few months, and mostly we'd just be working together, nothing else."

"Tiny little office space? Like, how tiny?" Danny leaned forward.

"Smaller than this living area." Adrian motioned around them. "Every time one of us had to turn around to look at the other's computer, our knees bumped. It wasn't exactly easy to avoid him. And since he's the head of the IT department, he's the one I had to work with most whenever we needed to figure something out."

"It's like it was fate."

"Or something." Adrian shook her head and then spent the next few minutes summing up how he roped her into singing at the banquet.

"So you actually went to the church event?"

Adrian nodded. "I did. I got to the parking lot and stood frozen outside for a few minutes. It'd been so long since I'd been back in a church building. He caught me right before I could leave and took me inside. I had a really good time, but it was awkward too. That night he introduced me as his friend. I hadn't realized we'd moved past coworker, so that caught me off guard."

Danny cocked her head to the side. "So, did you think of you guys as friends after that?"

"I'm not sure. I think I considered us more than coworkers but less than friends, if that makes sense." Adrian held up her hands to indicate where they fell on an invisible scale.

"Okay, so you guys went to the church thing, and then he just grew closer and closer?"

"I'm not sure how any of this happened, honestly. I mean, one minute I was trying to decide if we were friends or not, and the next I was trying my best not to think of him at all and not succeeding a bit. That's how he talked his way into coming to the Pyramid with me when you and the boys were here. I wanted to spend time with him, and I think I secretly wanted to know what you thought about him, too, to see if I was a complete nutcase."

Danny smirked. "You've always been a nutcase, but I also approved pretty much from the first moment I saw him. You're right about his smile. And there's just something about him that makes you feel like ... home." She gave Adrian a look that said she was studying her. "Is that the way he makes you feel?"

"I'm not sure what home feels like." Adrian shrugged. "But I'm glad you approve. He even helped me avoid a meltdown at the top of the Pyramid after you guys left."

"Wait! The top? You hate heights." Danny leaned back again.

"Tell me about it. I started freaking out almost the moment we got on the elevator, which you can see out of as you go up and down. My terror must've been pretty obvious because he wrapped his arm around me. I was still scared, but for some reason, I knew he wasn't going to let anything bad happen to me. And I felt better. Can you feel scared and better at the same time?" Adrian picked up her mug and headed back to the kitchen.

"Yeah. There've been several times I felt that way with Phil too."

Adrian poured another cup of coffee and doctored it up. "Then you got ahold of me during dinner. And the next thing I knew, I was headed to Sassafras. You were harsh to me that evening. I went to my room and thought, 'Wouldn't it be nice to have someone to help me through this like Danny has Phil?' And then he was there the next afternoon."

"Dad totally approves, by the way." Danny moved her feet out of the way as Adrian sat back down. "The fact that he'd drive several hours to pray over someone he didn't even know, he obviously cares about you—we could all see it when he glanced your way. And he chatted with Dad, took time to visit with others there, bent down to talk to the boys, everything—he just came across as a really great guy. When you'd both gone, Dad looked at me and said, 'I hope he catches her.'"

"He said that?" Adrian peeped over the rim of the mug.

"He said that." Danny got up and stretched, then grabbed a mug and finished off Adrian's pot of coffee. "So obviously more has happened between now and then because otherwise you wouldn't be this upset. Fill me in."

Adrian stood and walked to the window, glanced at the sky, then moved to lean against the table. She was antsy. "We started eating lunch together. Every day. He'd ask me about my past, and piece by piece, I filled him in on our moves, how we never knew who to trust because someone might convince the elders they needed to ask Dad to leave again. How I couldn't let myself make close friends because I didn't want to have to deal with the pain of leaving them."

"I don't even think you've talked to me about all of that." Danny moved over and leaned against the table next to her.

"I didn't figure I had to. I mean, you lived through the same thing I did."

Danny tilted her head. "Yes, but that doesn't mean it was exactly the same for me. I wish you'd talked to me before now."

"You're getting into what I wanted to ask you. Do you want me to ask you now or keep telling about Gray?" Adrian raised an eyebrow.

Danny wrinkled her nose. "That's totally not fair. Now I'm really curious about the question, but I still want to hear all about Gray. Okay. Finish that and then we'll delve into the other."

Okay. Onward. "Work got crazy, and we missed over a week's worth of lunches, but we ended up getting the afternoon off for the Fourth of July—"

"Wasn't that a Sunday?"

"Yeah, but we'd been working crazy hours because we'd just launched the new software. I figured I'd be in the office at least part of that day, so it was nice to have it free." Adrian returned to the couch with Danny following. "Gray asked me to go with him to see the fireworks down by the river. I agreed."

"I bet that was gorgeous."

Adrian thought back but couldn't remember much about what the fireworks had looked like, so she just nodded. "That night, I told him about how we'd had to move the summer before senior year. About how mean people were, about how I couldn't trust anyone, about how my faith in God ... well, it basically stopped." She closed her eyes and could picture that night again, how close they were, his arm behind her back, his hand against her cheek.

"He kissed you!" Danny hit the couch, making Adrian's eyes pop back open.

"How did you know?"

"The dreamy look on your face, the way your hand touched your cheek. You were remembering. Was it just out of the blue?"

Adrian thought back. "Sort of. One minute he was telling me to not give up faith in God just because people had hurt me. The fireworks started. He brushed my hair back, pulled me closer, and the next thing I knew, our lips were touching."

A huge sigh escaped Danny as she sat back. "Wow."

For another moment, Adrian stayed in the memory before jerking herself back to the here-and-now. "We didn't talk much more that evening. I almost wondered if he regretted it. And he was fairly normal at work the next day, too, whereas I was crazy. Brad sent me to other offices for a few days, though, and I kept busy, trying not to dwell on it. Then Thursday evening Gray asked me out on a date. Said he had a surprise for me."

"You hate surprises."

Adrian nodded. "This one was perfect, though. We went to the drive-in theater. He pulled ice cream out of a cooler and made sundaes. And the movie that was showing was *Meet Me in St. Louis*."

"Wow. Totally perfect." Danny held up her hands. "Seriously, what's the problem?"

Adrian drew her knees up to her chest and hugged them. "He told me he wanted a relationship when he dropped me off that night. I told him I couldn't."

"What? Adie, why?"

"We live in different states, for one. I'm only here for about another week. He deserves better, for a third." Adrian ticked each reason off on her fingers.

Danny grabbed her hand and shook it. "No. There is no one better than you. And the rest can be worked out."

"He said, 'God can work things out if we want them to work.'" Adrian felt the tears starting to well up behind her eyes again. "He deserves a girl who can believe that."

17

Danny stared silently at Adrian for a few moments. "You said you had a question for me."

The lump in Adrian's throat took a few swallows to remove. "You keep talking about how we're twins—we have a connection. Like we said a little bit ago, we went through the same things growing up. And yet, we turned out so differently."

"Right. Just because our DNA is the same, it doesn't mean we're exactly alike. But that's not a question."

Adrian pointed to Danny. "Why did we turn out so differently, though? Why do you still have a solid faith in God, and I can't even bear to set foot in a church building?"

Danny leaned back, a small crease between her eyebrows as she thought. "I'm not sure exactly what made us turn out differently. I mean, we've always had slightly different personalities. Mom used to say you had an 'old soul.'

"You would make friends more easily with the older people in the congregations, you loved old movies, you'd rather curl up with a book than go out and be social. I, on the other hand, would much rather go out and attend a party or go bowling with friends, and while I like old movies, I'm not obsessed with them like you."

"I'm not obsessed."

Danny raised an eyebrow. "Debatable. Anyway, I guess my personality made it easier for me to make friends with people our age. We also had other different interests—you loved computers and math. I loved English and art. That meant we hung out with different people in school too. And as we got older, it seemed like you didn't even try to make friends much, like you just wanted to keep to yourself."

"Can you blame me?" Adrian crossed her legs. "I mean, what's the point of trying to make friends if we're just going to have to leave again? They might say they'll be pen pals or keep up online, but you know that's not going to last much longer than one letter each."

"So you tried to guard your heart."

"I tried. I let my guard down a bit the last few years we were in Tennessee. We'd been there longer than any other place, and I got more comfortable. And look how that backfired."

Danny leaned forward and touched her knee. "I'm not sure I'd call it backfired. It made those years in Tennessee easier on you because you had friends. It's normal to have friends."

"Now you're saying I'm not normal."

"You've never been normal. I'm the normal twin." Danny winked. "But seriously, you kept looking at it as potential heartbreak. I guess I thought it was more like more people I won't have to introduce myself to in Heaven because I'll already know them. And I do keep up with several of them online still. We share pictures and stuff. It's not quite as desperate as you think."

Pushing off the sofa, Adrian paced. "You're okay with not seeing people again this side of Heaven like it's no big deal. That's pretty morbid."

Danny shook her head. "It's not morbid. It's something to look forward to. Besides, if I let it eat me up, I'd end up like you —no home, no friends, no hope."

Adrian stopped her pacing for a second and shot a glare at her sister. "Wow. Thanks. Way to make me feel better."

"I'm not sure you can feel better yet. You've been holding all this inside so long it's started festering, and maybe we need to drain the bad out before the good can take its place."

"Eww."

"Yeah, well, sorry. That's the analogy I have right now because I've been dealing with an infected mosquito bite on Seth. It's what's on my brain."

Adrian wrinkled her nose. "Again, ew."

"Yeah. That's motherhood." Danny propped her feet up on the coffee table. "But, seriously, that can't be what's kept you from church. The fear of making friends you'll have to leave again isn't enough to keep someone away from God."

Adrian sighed. "It's part of it. I just ... I guess I feel so betrayed by God. I mean, everyone talks about how good He is, how He will answer your prayers and take care of you, but all He's ever done is take me away from all I've ever known. Then we'd move to a new place and have to start all over.

"And I'd look at all those people who were supposed to be my church family and wonder which one would get upset with Dad and throw the fit that made the elders ask Dad to move us again. I could never relax. I could never feel like they were family."

"You keep saying that—that you wondered who you could trust. What are you talking about?"

"Remember how Dad would tell us we had to move again? And I would ask him why. Several times, it was because some people in the church got upset about something to do with him and convinced the elders that he didn't need to be the preacher there anymore.

"But we'd never find out who complained. Or what their issue with Dad was. We'd just have to pack up our lives and go start over somewhere else. I mean, how do you not go to church those last few weeks and wonder which ones ruined your life?"

"You do realize the church is made up of humans and humans

aren't perfect, right? I know we're supposed to strive for perfection as Christians, but that doesn't mean any of us actually reach it."

"But Christians are supposed to be loving and put others before themselves and look out for each other. You shouldn't have to feel like you have to walk on eggshells around them just to be accepted. Not that I ever really felt accepted by the kids at church. We were basically outcasts because we were the preacher's daughters." Adrian shook her finger at her sister.

"Yeah, okay. We weren't readily accepted by the youth group. That's why I made friends at summer camp and the local youth events and school. And I just tried to show God's love to the ones who didn't show it to me, because how else will they know how to if they never see it?"

If Adrian walked back and forth much more, she'd wear a spot in the carpet. "Fine, so you're a better person than I am. I still don't know if I can trust anyone at church again. I mean, all those people we worshipped with growing up seemed great when we first moved there. You never knew they would eventually stab you in the back. I can't go be a part of that."

Danny stood up and stopped Adrian's pacing. "They're not all like that."

Adrian gave her a skeptical look.

"Seriously. Did you talk to any of the church members who visited Dad while he was in the hospital?"

"Not really."

"Did you know they're taking care of Dad and Mom right now, making sure he doesn't overdo it with work so that he can heal? Did you know they're not cutting his salary through all of this even though he's not preaching full-time yet, and they even took up a special collection to help with medical bills?"

Adrian opened and closed her mouth. What could she say?

Danny gave Adrian a little shake. "And look at Gray and his friends. They're Christians. Do you think they're going to stab you in the back?"

"I don't know Gray's friends very well." Adrian knew it was a weak argument, but she was floundering.

"Are you kidding me? They drove to Arkansas to visit Dad while he was in the hospital, and they didn't even know him!" Danny threw her hands up in disgust. "What about me? And Mom and Dad? We're Christians. Are we going to stab you in the back? What about Phil?"

"Danny, that's not fair."

"No, Adrian." Danny poked her in the shoulder. "What's not fair is you're trying to judge all Christians by what a few did when we were growing up. Just like you and I are not the same, not all Christians are the same either." Danny walked into the bedroom and Adrian heard the bathroom door shut.

Back in the kitchen, Adrian dumped the coffee grounds from the coffeemaker and rinsed out the carafe. She leaned against the counter and tried to catch her breath. Why couldn't her sister understand? Except Adrian wasn't sure her own understanding was as clear as it had been before Danny had come today. A throat cleared beside her, and Adrian looked back up.

Danny leaned against the kitchen doorway. "I heard this illustration once, and I think maybe it will give you something else to think about. You have a carrot, an egg, and some coffee. Put each into a pot of boiling water and see what happens. The carrot softens, the egg hardens, but the coffee gets stronger. It's the same water. You and I went through the same things, but you chose to let it harden you. I prefer to think I let it make me stronger."

Adrian dried her hand on the towel. "So you think I'm hard?"

"I think you want to be hard. You push people away. You took this job where you can't stay anywhere very long so they don't have a chance to get to know you, to get too close. You bury yourself in books and movies instead of going out and living life. Now Gray has wiggled between a crack, you didn't even know was in your walls, and touched your heart, and you don't know what to do. Maybe it's time to try trusting again."

ADRIAN SAT STILL long after Danny left early that afternoon. They hadn't talked much more about anything of importance for the rest of their time together, but their main discussion ran on repeat through Adrian's head. What was she missing? Did she want to be an egg? She'd always considered herself more like her drink of choice.

She opened her computer and checked her email to make sure she hadn't missed any help requests—nothing new. She glanced at the clock, only two-thirty in the afternoon. Without letting herself overthink it, she picked up her phone and pushed the rarely used contact.

"Mom? Would it be all right if I come and spend the night?"

"Of course." Not a hint of hesitation tinged her mother's voice.

It only took a few minutes to throw some clothes in a bag and point her car west. *What am I doing? This is ridiculous. I don't even know what to say.*

Now instead of the discussion with her sister, Dad's words from the hospital were ringing through her head again, and she couldn't resist the urge to go and tell him she didn't blame him. Maybe that was strange, considering none of the things that hurt her would've happened if he hadn't been a preacher in the first place. But she couldn't hold it against him. She understood the urge to follow a job you loved, even if it came with a less-than-ideal lifestyle.

She crossed the river and gripped her steering wheel a little tighter, keeping it pointed in the right direction. Had she let her circumstances harden her? An egg? She didn't even like eggs that much. She shook her head. The analogy made some sense, but she couldn't think of herself as hard. She could still laugh and sing—that meant she had a soft side, right?

It was almost dinner time when she walked in the back door of her parents' home. Mom looked up from stirring something on the stove. She turned the burner off, came over, and wrapped Adrian in a hug.

"I'm so glad you came, even if it's only for a little while. Everything okay?" She brushed Adrian's hair back behind her ears.

"It's okay, Mom. I just wanted to talk to Dad, and work has been insane, so a trip away for a little while sounded good."

"Hey, A." Dad walked in from the den, looking better than he had several weeks before. He was a bit thinner but otherwise appeared as though he wasn't recovering from a life-threatening situation.

"Dad." Adrian went and gave him the first real hug she'd given him in years, not allowing him to get by with an awkward side-hug this time. "You're looking better."

He gave her a look as though to make sure she really was Adrian and not Danielle. "Thanks. I'm feeling much better. If your mother would ease up on me, it would be like nothing had happened."

"But something did happen. And that means we can't act like it didn't. Otherwise, it might happen again." Mom carried a couple of dishes to the table, enticing Adrian with their aromas. "Go wash up so we can eat."

At the table, Adrian sat beside Dad and across from Mom. They joined hands, and Adrian bowed her head for the first time in years as her father blessed the food.

"We thank you, God, for bringing Adrian to us this weekend. Thank you for our health and for this good food we're about to partake. Be with us through the rest of the weekend and tomorrow as we worship you. And please keep Adrian safe as she travels home tomorrow. We love you, Lord. In Jesus' name, Amen."

Dad gave her hand a slight squeeze before he let go and dished up green beans. It was a gesture she'd felt most of her life, one she'd come to consider a necessity for the end of a prayer. One Gray had also done when they prayed at the end of the banquet. She chased thoughts of Gray from her head and scooped out some mashed potatoes.

Dinner conversation revolved around inconsequential things: talk about her Memphis position almost being done, news Dad was back to preaching tomorrow for the first time since his heart attack, a report from Mom on how many zucchinis she was getting from her garden. A few stories of Danielle's boys made them all laugh. Even though there was still some tension between them, it didn't seem quite as thick as it had been.

"I need to go check the thermostat at the church building. Want to walk with me?" Dad pulled on his tennis shoes in the mudroom.

"Sure. If Mom doesn't need help cleaning up."

Mom waved her off as she loaded the dishwasher. "I've been doing it myself for longer than you've been alive. Pretty sure I can handle it tonight too."

The church building was just up the block from the house. She and Dad meandered down the driveway and through the quiet neighborhood. How many times had she walked this exact way with this man who used to be her primary confidante? Now she was just a couple of inches shorter than he was. Their strides were similar, their arms swinging in a rhythm.

He unlocked the side door and pulled it open. Hesitant to cross the threshold after so long, she paused for a moment. He tilted his head, gave her a questioning look. Squaring her shoulders and taking a breath, she stepped into the dark interior. The smell of wood pews, old songbooks, and lemon-scented cleaner filled her nose. Dad flipped on the lights.

The bulletin board in the foyer had a little human figure standing on one side and a big figure on the other side marked 'God.' The words said, "When you feel far from God, ask yourself, 'Who moved?'"

She swallowed a lump. God wasn't going to strike her dead for being here with so many questions. Even if she was still mad at Him.

Dad led the way down the hallway and readjusted the thermostat so the building would be comfortable in the morning. Some of the little old ladies would still think it was too cold, but they all kept their personal afghans draped on the pew where they always sat. Her footsteps echoed on the linoleum as they returned to the front part of the building.

Flipping on the light in his office, Dad stepped to his desk and waved at the wingchair. "Have a seat for a minute. I've got to get a few things together for tomorrow."

This chair had been hers for as long as she could remember. On a bad day growing up, she'd escape to Daddy's office and talk to the best listener she knew. When had she quit thinking of him that way? She curled her legs underneath her while he shuffled through papers and notebooks. His desk was always a mess—he and Gray were similar in that way for sure.

"So do I dare ask what brought you here tonight? I can't imagine you coming for no reason. You aren't like Danielle in that aspect." Dad perched himself on the edge of his desk chair and glanced at her from over his glasses.

Maybe it was the chair. Maybe it was the talk with Danny earlier that day. Maybe it was something completely different. But she finally wanted to talk to him.

"I don't blame you."

He looked up again from the papers he'd been straightening.

"When I came down, and you were in the hospital, you said you wished you could've done something different for me as we grew up. I could tell you were blaming yourself for me having issues with God." She shook her head. "But I don't."

"Adrian, that's all well and good, but it doesn't explain why you've made yourself a stranger for the last four years."

Adrian untucked her legs from beneath her. "It was too hard to be here. Mom always thinks she has to say something about me coming to church again. You avoid the topic like the plague, which just makes it a bigger elephant in the room. And I do stay busy with my job."

"I figured you stayed so busy with work for the same reason you avoided us."

Her head tilted in concession. "Maybe. My sister said the same thing earlier today when she came and forced me to talk to her."

"Oh?"

Shifting in her seat, she got a little more comfortable. "She showed up in Memphis and said she wasn't leaving until I opened up some. It wasn't comfortable, but it made me want to come talk to you a little too. And make sure you knew I don't blame you."

"So, who do you blame?" He leaned forward, his elbows on the desk.

"God, foremost, probably. After all, He let all of this happen to us."

"Okay. God can take it. What else?"

Adrian frowned. "Really? That's all you're going to say about that? You're not going to try to tell me I'm a horrible person for blaming God for my problems?"

"Job did. David did. You're not exactly the first person to blame God for what goes on in your life. You're forgetting that just because something bad happens doesn't mean something good can't come from it." He pointed at her. "If you hadn't had to move around so much growing up, you might not know how to cope with going to all these new places for your job now."

The thought stilled her, catching her off guard. She seemed to be having lots of those lately. But was he right? Had the past she'd blamed for everything actually prepared her for the life she'd taken on in adulthood?

She'd have to think more about that later. "Danny says I'm using my job to avoid having relationships with people. That it helps me keep my distance from things."

He seemed to consider that for a moment. "Probably. But that doesn't mean all those things you learned each time you had to find your way in a new place doesn't help you now. I'm sure it makes it easier to learn your way around a new town quickly. And it probably helps you have the ability to jump into a new situation and just get up there and do your job instead of being shy about being in front of people you've never met before."

"I guess." Adrian shrugged. "But still, God let those people have whatever issues with you and talk the elders into firing you. I mean, aren't Christians supposed to be loving and nonjudgmental and better than other people? How could they just uproot our lives like that?"

Her father held his hands up. "Wait, wait, wait. Is that what you think? That someone 'got' us fired?"

Adrian threw herself back in the chair in exasperation. "Well what else could I think? You came home and told us that the elders told you they wanted a new preacher and we needed to leave. When I asked you about it later, you said they'd told you that several people had come to them with issues they were having with you. So yes. They got you fired."

"No. That's not the whole story. And that only happened once or twice." He shook his head. "Is *that* why you've been refusing to come to church services?"

"I never know who I can trust. The rest of the time we were in Tennessee, I'd look around and wonder who it was who'd had issues with you and wonder if they felt guilty about me having to move right before my senior year."

Her dad leaned back in his chair and sighed. "Adrian, that's a very oversimplified way to look at it." He ran a hand through his thinning hair. "Yes, in that instance, several people had gone to the elders about some problems they were having. But I wasn't at the root of all of them. And most of the problems the elders decided might be fixed if they got someone new in the pulpit. It wasn't personal. They had to take what was given to them and make the best decision they could for everyone involved."

"But it wasn't the best decision for us!" Adrian hit her fists against the armrests of the chair.

"Actually, I think it was. You'd never really been happy there.

Yes, in the end, you'd made a few friends, but a lot of those kids treated you like an outcast the whole time because you hadn't lived there your whole life. It's stupid, but it's the way kids act sometimes." He motioned around his office.

"And this was a great move for us. The kids here seemed more accepting, I've been able to get more involved in local activities, which has helped the church have some outreach and bring some others to God, the whole congregation has opened their arms to our family and taken care of us—especially lately— and your mother seems to be the happiest she's been in a while."

Adrian wanted to argue, but she couldn't deny any of what her father had just said.

"No, it's not been easy to move around, to see you girls having to readjust and relearn and find a place in a new location. But you've done it every time, and you've done it well. Like it or not, it's shaped who you've become, and that's not a bad thing. You're strong and independent and capable."

Adrian shook her head. "Danny thinks I'm hard, not strong."

One of his eyebrows rose in question.

"She said that if you put an egg, a carrot, and coffee all in boiling water, one will come out hard, one soft, and one strong. She said the water is the same, but how we react to it is different. She compared herself to the coffee and me to the egg."

He pursed his lips as he seemed to consider that. "I guess that's a pretty good application. Let's try this one instead, though. The same sun that melts the wax hardens the clay. It's along the same lines of thought but a little different. And I agree with your sister; you're almost an ideal example of an experiment. Your DNA is the same, but you both turned out completely different even though you grew up in the same household and went through pretty much the same things."

"So am I supposed to be the wax or the clay?"

He shrugged. "I don't think it matters. I think as long as you understand that you can choose how you come out of a trial, you've got the lesson." He stood. "Your mother will be wondering what's become of us."

She walked with him as he turned off the lights and locked the door again. "I just wanted to make sure you knew I didn't blame you."

Clasping her hand, he gazed at her in the evening light. "I appreciate that, but I also think your blame is mislaid. It sounds like as much as you say you blame God, you're also blaming your fellow Christians. You think they judged our family wrongly. You think they were unfair and unjust."

She waited without replying, unable to deny what he was saying. It rang true in her ears.

He shook his head. "Aren't you doing something similar? You don't even know who went to the elders in the first place, but instead of giving everyone the benefit of doubt, you're holding them all responsible. You're not giving anyone a chance to prove themselves to be a true Christian, a friend who loves you no matter what. And you're not forgiving anyone either.

"You're holding this all in your heart and letting it eat at you instead of letting it go and growing from it." He walked with her a little farther down the street before he stopped once more. "I just don't think you'll find the peace you're looking for until you admit you're no better than the people you've been blaming all these years."

Squeezing her hand, he walked into the house without another word. She sat on the back steps for a little while, watching the sun go down over the rice field behind the yard. Fireflies danced under the pecan tree, and a mourning dove cried a few times nearby. So much had happened today, and she wasn't sure what to do with any of it.

Am I wrong? Have I been wrong all these years? How do I fix this?

18

Where was she? Gray checked his phone again, but there was no response from the last three messages he'd sent. It wasn't like Adrian to not reply within minutes of getting a text.

Had something happened? Surely she wasn't still asleep, despite their crazy hours yesterday. And he didn't have another way of contacting her or anyone else in her life to check on her.

He returned his focus to the computer screen, trying to understand what the IT guy in St. Louis was telling him to do, but he was slower than Adrian would be about knowing where to look. It was probably as frustrating to the tech as it was to him.

"It's almost nine o'clock. I don't think we're going to get anything else done tonight, especially without having Adrian here." Diane sighed. "Why don't we just plan to reconvene in the morning, and hopefully we'll hear back from her by then."

Gray swallowed his disappointment that he'd have to miss worship services. Since it was his weekend to be on call, he'd known this was a possibility, but that didn't bother him any less. He nodded, signed off from the online chat, and closed everything down.

"Maybe God will pull some strings overnight, and when we

try again tomorrow, it will all work like it did when we left Friday evening."

"From your lips to God's ears, Gray." Diane bid him goodnight and headed to her car.

Gray sent up several prayers as he drove home. For the work situation. But also for Adrian, wherever she was. Something inside him said she was going through something right now, and he hated that he wasn't there to help. He sent a quick text to Mom.

Don't plan on me for lunch tomorrow. Have to work.

His phone rang less than a minute later.

"What's going on? You missed lunch a few weeks ago, and now you're missing again?" Her voice was more concerned than chiding.

"It's my weekend to be on call, and we had some issues come up today that we didn't get fixed. So I'll need to go in tomorrow morning and make sure everything gets squared away for payroll before I can do anything else." He kicked off his shoes, not caring where they landed.

"I thought you said Adrian would have everything working fine."

"We thought she did when we left last night. But something else happened again today when they pulled the final reports. And we can't get ahold of Adrian on the phone." He ran his fingers through his hair, grimacing when he tugged too hard.

"You can't get ahold of her? Is she okay?"

"If I could reach her, I'd be able to answer that." He rolled his eyes, grateful Mom couldn't see it.

"Gray, I'm praying. You keep us updated, okay?"

"Of course."

"Love you."

"Love you too."

"Have you told her your story yet?" Mom's question stopped him right as he was about to hang up.

"Not yet."

"You need to tell her. She needs to hear it from you."

"I know. It's her last week here. I'm hoping I can find the time."

"I'll pray for that too."

When Mom promised to pray, she didn't mean sending a few quick sentences Heavenward. Instead, she'd spend hours on her knees, laying it all out before their Heavenly Father, praising, thanking, and beseeching. He needed to follow suit. Despite how exhausted he was after the last few days, he wouldn't rest until he'd fully laid everything out before the Lord.

Including asking God to show him when and how to tell Adrian about his past. Whether it made a difference or not, she needed to know he wasn't perfect.

———

"YOUR PHONE WAS BEEPING." Mom glanced up from the book she was reading when Adrian finally came in.

"Oh, thanks." Adrian checked and saw several text messages from the office. The reports she thought they'd fixed yesterday messed up again, and they needed them perfect by eight o'clock on Monday. "I guess I'm heading back to Memphis early." She held up the phone. "Problems with payroll."

"Oh no." Mom placed a bookmark between the pages and set the novel aside. "Will you have to drive back tonight?"

A glance at the clock made Adrian grimace. "It's late enough I don't want to even try. No one is at the office at this hour anyway. I'll get up early in the morning and just head straight there."

Mom frowned. "I was hoping you'd be able to come to church with us."

Adrian paused for a moment. "Maybe next time. Guess I

better turn in for the night since I'm up early tomorrow." She kissed Mom's cheek and then headed to bed. It was unlikely she'd get much rest after everything that had happened over the last few days. But something about the familiar bed, the sound of a train several blocks away whistling its way through town, Dad's snores down the hall, all seemed to work as a lullaby and rocked her to sleep.

———

THE NEXT MORNING, Dad was in the living room, his head bent over his sermon notes, the glow of the lamp illuminating him in his early studies. He looked up as she walked into the room, her duffel slung over her shoulder. She tiptoed over to him and kissed his cheek.

"Work calls." She shifted the strap as it dug into her collar bone.

"Me too." He grinned at her as he pointed to his papers.

"I'll call you soon."

"Please do. I miss our talks."

She ducked her head. "Me too. Love you. Tell Mom goodbye for me, please?"

"Sure."

Driving east early in the day had one major problem: the sun was in a horrible position. She squinted against it as she made her way past fields and small towns and headed toward the river. How many times had she crossed this river in the last few months? Was it only a few? It seemed like millions.

The Pyramid stood sentinel as she came into Memphis, rays shining off its glass sides. Traffic was sparse this early on a Sunday morning, and she easily made her way to the office. Only three cars were in the parking lot, one being Gray's. She punched in the access code she'd been given and heard the door click unlocked.

Weaving her way through the quiet building, she headed to

the corner Accounting occupied. "Sorry I missed those texts yesterday. I was driving and then forgot to take my phone with me yesterday evening."

"It's a huge mess." Diane studied a computer screen next to Gray.

"Of course it is." Adrian set her bag down on the extra chair in the room and came over to look. She grimaced as she saw that all the work they'd done Friday seemed to have been put in a blender, chopped to pieces, and rearranged in a random order on the screen. "Okay. Let's see if we can figure out what's going on."

GRAY STOOD up to make way for her to sit down.

"If you need to leave for church, Gray, we'll hold down the fort until you get back." Adrian's voice didn't sound accusatory or haughty. Had she really meant that?

She clicked through several things and signed in under her username on the software.

"I can just go to evening services if you need me." He leaned against the wall.

"It's up to you." She glanced over at him. "It will take me a while to dig around in here and try to determine why it looks like this."

"It wouldn't be fair to you." He shrugged, refusing to show her any sign of emotion. "I'm in it for the long haul."

Adrian glanced back up at him again. Could she tell he meant not only about the job but about her too? He met her eyes for only a moment before looking over her shoulder at Diane.

"Do you need to run and do anything, Diane?"

"There won't be much you can do with payroll until I can figure a few things out." Adrian turned to face the head of Accounting.

"I could stand to run and get some breakfast. I didn't eat

anything on my way here this morning." Diane grabbed her purse. "I'll be back. Thanks."

"Sure." Adrian frowned as she studied the programming language on the screen in front of her. She pulled up a chat box with an IT guy back in St. Louis to run some ideas past him as she delved into the situation.

Coffee. She probably wanted coffee. He slipped out of the room and brewed a pot. Why they hadn't done it before now, he didn't know. He guesstimated the amounts of creamer for hers and hoped he got them right. He ought to know after seeing her make so many cups this summer.

Sliding into the chair beside her, Gray set her coffee nearby but stayed several inches away.

Did she miss the accidental bumps they'd shared in their little basement office? Did she miss being friends and not just coworkers? He did. No time to talk through such things now.

"Daddy should be starting his sermon in a few minutes, depending on how many songs the leader picked out to sing this morning." She pointed to the time at the bottom of her screen. "I didn't get a chance to find out what the topic was before I left."

Gray looked at her instead of the computer. "You were in Arkansas?"

"I drove down yesterday afternoon after Danny left."

"Danny was here?" He'd missed a lot, evidently.

"She came to tell me I was the weird twin and she was the normal one." Adrian glanced over at him. "Among other things."

Was that a special twin code or something? "What?"

Adrian sat back as the IT guy took over her screen through his computer back in St. Louis. Her mouse scrolled over the screen as if it had a mind of its own, clicking open windows, highlighting text, running a couple of scans.

"She came and cornered me without permission because she thought something was wrong. We ended up really talking for the first time in a while. I guess all those times I thought

I'd spoken to her in the past few years, I was really just chatting about little stuff but never touched on the real problems."

As she relayed the events of the day before, he studied her. Although she appeared tired, she didn't seem as stressed or emotional as she had. Like something had lifted from her shoulders. And conversing with her sister had done that—not something he'd done.

"She basically told me I was being unfair and judgmental, hard and stand-offish, stupid."

The hero in him rose, begging to defend her. "You're not stupid. Or hard."

Her grin gave away the fact he didn't include the other bad things. "Yeah, well, I guess it depends on who I'm around. Anyway, she got me thinking more than I've let myself in the last few years, and I decided to go make sure my dad knew I didn't blame him for anything that happened. We really talked last night. Something I missed like nothing else."

Gray started to reach for her but then pulled back at the last second. "And he was glad to hear you weren't blaming him?"

"No." She answered the question on the chat window before she looked at Gray again. "He told me my blame was misplaced."

Same thing Gray had told her a few weeks before. "So, who are you supposed to blame?"

"I guess no one."

Before they could talk anymore, her phone buzzed. The IT guy was calling to talk her through something he couldn't get to work on his end to see if she could make it happen on hers. She put the call on speaker and clicked through the steps as he said them, with Gray pointing out a few things he noticed as they went.

By lunch, they'd isolated what was causing the issue, but the IT guy needed to fix a few things in St. Louis before anything else could be done in Memphis. Adrian leaned back and stretched. She tilted her head to each side as if easing up a kink in the middle of her shoulders. He'd offer to rub it for her, but it was safer if he didn't.

"Sorry you had to work on a Sunday." She glanced his way. "I know you don't usually miss church services."

"It was my weekend to be on call. Just the way things go sometimes. Besides, I'm planning to slip out for an hour and make it to Bible study this evening if I can."

Several unreadable emotions flitted across Adrian's face for a moment before her gaze met his. "Mind if I join you?"

He blinked. Was he dreaming? Had he fallen asleep while waiting for her to get things fixed?

Adrian glanced back at the computer screen. "Oh. No. I probably can't get away anyway. I mean, Diane will probably need me to stay here. I'm not sure what I was thinking."

"No." Gray reached out and touched her shoulder. "Sorry. You just caught me off guard. I'm thinking once we get this report fixed, Diane probably won't need you anymore today. Of course, you're more than welcome to go with me."

Adrian glanced at him and then down at her lap. "Okay. We'll see what Diane needs from me and if I can get away or not."

Lord, please let Diane not need her this evening. And if this works out, help me find a way to tell her my story too.

DIANE PRACTICALLY JUMPED up and down when she came in that afternoon and saw the report looking the way it should. Adrian grinned. Gray had gone downstairs to check something on his computer, so she was the only one to enjoy the absolute glee on the accounting head's face.

"I'll still need to fiddle with it some this week to make sure it runs correctly from here on out. This was the first time we've worked with the company who runs your payroll software, so we weren't sure how it would go, but we think we've figured out how to get our program to talk to theirs now." Adrian waved at the screen. "I'll run some more tests over the next few days to make certain we have it completely up to par."

Diane ran her finger down the screen, following the two columns of numbers. "This is great. This is exactly what we needed. Maybe we can knock out the paychecks tonight and get them mailed first thing in the morning."

"Is there any other way I can help you?" Adrian leaned against the edge of the desk.

"No. I think we're good. Basically, I'll get my teammates together, and we'll scan through everything to make sure it matches, fix the few that don't, and send it to the printer." Diane tapped her pencil against her mouse pad. "Thanks so much for coming in. Gray said you drove in from Arkansas this morning."

"Yeah, it's okay. It had been a spur-of-the-moment thing, so I wasn't surprised when I had to cut it a little short." Adrian shrugged. "It worked out."

Gray poked his head in the doorway. "Everything good?"

"It's looking perfect." Diane beamed at him. "I'm about to get Chris and Stacy in here and knock this out so we can get checks mailed in the morning."

"Sounds good. Do you need us to stick around for anything else right now? You can still get ahold of us with our phones, of course." Gray tapped his fingers against the doorframe.

"No. You guys should go enjoy what's left of the weekend." Diane waved her hand to shoo them away.

Adrian gathered her things and walked beside Gray through the mostly silent building. They didn't talk. Or touch. Or glance each other's way. He held the door open for her as they exited into the hot, humid July afternoon. She shielded her eyes with her hand until she could adjust to the change in brightness.

"We've still got a couple hours before the church service starts." Gray walked beside her through the parking lot.

"Do you want me to just meet you there?" Adrian pushed the button on her key fob to unlock her car.

"I could pick you up—if you wanted." He twisted his keychain around and around in his hand.

"Sure. That would be great. Do I need to dress up?"

He took in what she was wearing. "No. We're pretty relaxed on Sunday evenings. Jeans are fine."

"See you in a bit, then." She drove back to her hotel, not sure what she'd just agreed to. On one hand, she was glad she'd asked to join him. On the other, she was terrified. Was she hoping to be proven wrong? Was she hoping to be proven right?

She pulled some ice cream out of the freezer and grabbed a spoon. Maybe a novel and something sweet would help calm her nerves. She let the velvety smoothness of the brownie-batter-flavored chocolate sit on her tongue for a moment before swallowing.

Her toenail polish was chipped. Should she repaint them or leave them alone for another day or two? She skimmed a few pages of the book she'd been reading but couldn't focus on the characters' problems when her own were so much more real.

ALL DAY LONG, the only thing that helped Gray through was knowing Mom was praying for him. And for Adrian. When she'd asked to go to worship with him this evening, it had taken all his willpower not to jump up and shout.

"Mom." Gray pressed his phone to his ear.

"Gray. Is everything okay now?"

"I think maybe it's getting there." He grinned. "She asked to come with me tonight. To the evening worship service."

"Gray ..." Mom's voice choked up. "That's definitely an answer to prayers."

"Yes. I wanted to give you a heads up because I haven't told her my story yet. I plan to after services."

"You aren't ready for her to meet us. To see how different we look." Mom's voice was matter-of-fact but not hurt. He grinned a bit at the thought of her introducing herself as his mother with her dark brown skin and black hair next to his fair complexion and blonde hair.

"I just need to prepare her first."

"I know, honey." Mom's love came through even in the way she talked. "We won't rush up and say, 'Hey,' unless you wave us to come on."

"Thanks." He grinned. "You know I love you."

"You better. Otherwise, I'd have to go back and raise you again just to make sure I got it right that time."

He chuckled. "See you this evening even if we don't talk."

"Maybe after she hears your story, you could bring her over for dinner one night this week." His mama's love language was food, and she was good at it.

"I'll try, Mom."

"We'll be praying God gives you the words you need to let her see the hurt still healing inside of you too."

A FEW MINUTES before Gray was supposed to pick her up, Adrian slipped into a dressier shirt even though he'd said she looked fine. After running a brush through her hair, she pulled it into a quick French braid, slipped on some wedge sandals, and applied a coat of lip gloss, then checked her reflection. Nice, but also terrified.

Deep breath. Squared shoulders. *I grew up going to church. It's not like it's something I can forget how to do.*

A light knock on the door made her jump a bit. When she opened it, Gray stood on the other side and studied her for a moment. Then he smiled, and she couldn't help but reciprocate.

"Ready?" He held out his hand.

After only a moment's hesitation, she placed her hand in his and nodded. "As I'm going to be."

175

"I'm glad you're joining me tonight." He held his car door open for her.

"I'm not making any promises for the future." She turned to look at him as they drove through town. "This is just for tonight right now. I'm doing a lot of ... well, I guess you could call it soul-searching. And I'm not even really sure why I agreed to this in the first place."

"No pressure." He tapped his fingers on the steering wheel as he waited to turn into the parking lot. "I just wanted you to know I'm glad you're coming tonight."

She walked beside him, this time toward the main church building instead of the fellowship hall. Several other people greeted Gray as they headed the same direction. Gray pulled the glass door open and held it for her. She took a deep breath and followed him in.

19

The preacher read from Psalm 139. "O Lord, You have searched me and known me. You know my sitting down and my rising up; You understand my thought afar off. You comprehend my path and my lying down, and are acquainted with all my ways. For there is not a word on my tongue, but behold, O Lord, You know it altogether."

Adrian had been away from church for over four years now. She hadn't considered herself hiding from God, but she also hadn't thought about the fact that He knew exactly where she was through it all. She knew she hadn't wanted to talk to Him or face Him or ... forgive Him. But she likewise hadn't acknowledged the fact that God knew what she was thinking the whole time.

"Where can I go from Your Spirit? Or where can I flee from Your presence? If I ascend into heaven, You are there; If I make my bed in hell, behold, You are there. If I take the wings of the morning, and dwell in the uttermost parts of the sea, even there Your hand shall lead me, and Your right hand shall hold me."

The preacher looked up from his Bible. "That is an awesome thought. And I don't use the word *awesome* like teenagers use it all the time. I don't just mean it's cool or neat or, as they used to say when I was in school, radical."

The congregation gave a little chuckle.

"*Dictionary.com* says *awesome* means 'inspiring an overwhelming feeling of reverence, admiration, or fear.' Fear. Reverence. Do you think about those things when thinking about God? I know a lot of people want to think He's a big grandpa just sitting up there in heaven, looking down and waiting to give us what we want. After all, isn't that what love is? That's what children think love means. If you give them what they want, you must love them."

Adrian shifted in her seat. Had she been considering God that way? He didn't answer her prayers the way she wanted, so she decided He didn't love her?

"God doesn't have to give us anything. He's already given us much more than we deserve, more than we can think or imagine. And yet, He still chooses to bless us each day even more."

Did He really do that? Did He give her blessings each day? Adrian tried to think of all the problems she'd been claiming for years as ways she wasn't blessed, but after talking with Gray and Danielle and Dad, she knew she had more blessings than not.

"And how do we repay Him?" The minister paused and scanned the auditorium. "We do whatever we want. We forget that whatever we do, wherever we go, whatever we think, God is there, and He knows. He knows our hearts and minds. And He forgives us."

Adrian ducked her head, studying the fingers she'd folded in her lap. Gray's hand reached over and covered hers, giving it a squeeze. She glanced over at him, and he pressed her fingers tight again.

"We need to remember that God isn't just a grandpa. Yes, He loves us—more than any earthly grandpa ever could. But He also expects us to realize that He paid a huge price for us, and we don't need to squander it away. None of us is perfect."

That seemed to be the theme of what everyone was telling her this weekend.

"But that doesn't mean we can't strive for perfection." The minister wrapped up the sermon, but Adrian was thinking back through all he'd already said, as well as what Danny and Dad had told her yesterday. She stood out of habit as everyone around her rose to sing.

Christine and Victoria cornered her after the closing prayer. "Adrian, we're so glad you're here. Come get dinner with us!"

Before Adrian could respond, Gray leaned around her and interrupted. "Can we get a raincheck? I need to talk to Adrian about something tonight."

"Ooh. That sounds serious." Victoria propped her fist on a hip. "Are you in trouble?"

"Probably." Adrian gave a grin she hoped seemed sincere. Inside she worried a bit about what Gray wanted to discuss.

"Of course we can do a raincheck. Maybe next week?" Christine pointed to her head. "Then you can show us how to do our hair like yours was at the banquet."

"Maybe." Adrian nodded.

Back in Gray's car, Adrian played with the edge of her purse strap as he wove his way through traffic.

"I know a great place that sells crepes. Does that sound okay?" He glanced over at her before making a right-hand turn.

"Sure." She forced her hands to be still. "If you're going to continue the sermon, I'm not sure I want to hear it. At least not right now."

"Actually, I was going to tell you about me." He steered them into a parking lot and got out before she could wrap her mind around what he'd just said. *What's there to tell? You're perfect.*

They sat at a stone-topped table on the patio, a fan turning above them just enough to stir the thick summer air and make it not so miserable. She took a sip from her sweet tea and admired the tomato, basil, and mozzarella-filled crepe on her plate.

"Mind if I say a prayer?" He asked before she could take a bite.

She replaced her fork on the table and bowed her head.

"Father God, we thank You for this beautiful evening to enjoy, for new friendships, for family, and for Your church. Please help me have the right words tonight as I tell Adrian my story. Continue to be with her father and heal him the rest of the way so that he can carry on Your good work. And bless Adrian as she searches her soul. Help her find the answers she's looking for. In Jesus' name I pray, Amen."

"You forgot to bless the food." Adrian met his gaze, trying to lighten the mood. She was thoroughly curious about his past now. She couldn't imagine what he might tell her that would warrant a prayer like that.

"God knows we're thankful for this meal." He sliced off a bite of his mushroom and swiss cheese crepe and stuffed it in his mouth.

"I guess I still have my work cut out for me this last week of working here, huh?" Adrian did what she always did when things got awkward. She talked about what she knew best. Her eyes slid shut in appreciation for the goodness she'd just put in her mouth.

———

"ADRIAN, NO MORE TALK ABOUT WORK." Gray's words came out a bit harsher than he meant, but he was on edge. "And I know you're leaving soon. Of all the things I know about you, that is the one foremost in my mind. But tonight, I thought we'd focus on me, if you're okay with that. I think it's time you learned my story."

She pointed her plastic fork at him. "What could be so bad in your past that you have to build up to it like this?"

"What do you think my childhood was like?" He leaned back and chewed another bite.

"You grew up in Memphis your whole life." She waved her hands in the air. "You were brought up in the church. You were probably the most popular kid in your youth group."

"Well, you got two out of three correct."

"Okay, so maybe not the *most* popular kid in youth group, but one of them, right?" She laughed, but it sounded slightly strained.

"That's not the one you got wrong." He crossed his arms and waited.

"You didn't grow up in Memphis?"

"I've been in Memphis pretty much my whole life."

"You weren't brought up in the church? Then how could you be in the youth group?"

He leaned forward with his elbows on the table. "I was taken to church services for the first time when I was fourteen."

She didn't say anything, just blinked.

"That's when the Robertses took me in."

It was like watching all her preconceived notions fall from her eyes as what he'd just said sank in.

"Up to that point I was in various foster homes. And usually in trouble."

She shook her head. "What?"

"My parents left me when I was a baby. I got passed around, taken in, reprimanded, and treated like no one wanted me. Until the Robertses."

Adrian leaned forward too, her forehead a map of wrinkles.

"It was rough going at first." He dragged the tines of his fork through his dinner, mutilating the once-beautiful meal. "I was so used to feeling unwanted, like I was in the way or not worth anyone's time, that I really couldn't wrap my mind around the fact that this couple might actually want to care for me.

"Especially since I was a gangly, awkward fourteen-year-old boy. Most people want a baby or at least a very young child. I figured this couple was just taking me in as a foster child and couldn't sincerely consider adopting me after all that time.

Especially since it's unusual for people to adopt kids with a different color skin."

He eased back in his chair and closed his eyes. "She asked me what my favorite kind of cookie was ... and I didn't know. I mean, I'd had cookies but not enough to be able to answer a question like that, especially since most of them had been store-bought and not homemade.

"She made it her goal to find out. Every couple of days, I would get home from school and find a plate of a different kind of cookie waiting for me: chocolate chip, snickerdoodle, oatmeal raisin, peanut butter, you name it."

"So, did you come up with a favorite?" Adrian scraped up another bite of her crepe.

"I did." He paused a moment before telling her. "Chocolate chip."

She smiled. "That would have been my guess."

Was it because she knew him so well now or because he seemed like a simple guy? She wasn't revealing an answer. But he hadn't exactly given her ample opportunities to get to know him either.

She seemed to mull what he'd said over as they nibbled the last few bites of dinner. As good as the food was, in his distraction he'd barely tasted anything. She startled when he stood.

"Do you want anything else?" He motioned to her empty plate.

SHE PUSHED THE DISH AWAY. "No. Just to hear more of your story. I want to know how you got from that background to how you are now." Maybe if she could figure out how he turned out the way he did, she could apply it to her own life? But even if she couldn't, she was more than intrigued.

He took their dishes back inside and then settled across from her again. "The Robertses took me in and showed me that a fourteen-year-old who'd been abandoned early in life could be loved anyway. They actually had to force me to go to church with them the first few times.

"I'd been with some other families in the past who'd taken me to church with them, but they only did it because it was expected of them. The Robertses meant it when they went to worship services. They were involved and didn't just do Bible studies at the church building—they did one each night after dinner too."

Adrian listened. This was so different from what she'd expected when she imagined how his childhood had been. Christianity was so much a part of his life now, she couldn't fathom a time when he had to be coerced into attending services.

"They signed me up for baseball that first spring I was with them when they found out I had some interest in the sport. There was a boy on the team who also went to church with them, and I started getting to know him more. He invited me to some of the youth group events and got me more involved with some of the other kids.

"That, paired with all the Robertses did with their home devotionals, prayers, and living out what they preached, really touched me." He shook his head. "I never knew life could be like that."

"And the kids just readily accepted you?" Adrian leaned with her elbows on the table, her chin on one fist. If they had, she wanted to know his secret. Or maybe not. There wasn't any way to go back into her past and change things—had she even wanted to try.

"Mostly. Not all of them at first because I was so ugly and awkward and a total mess. I thought I was a bad boy, I guess. And I was different. They weren't used to being around someone who'd been through what I had."

"I can't imagine you being ugly." She gave a little laugh.

"So you don't think I'm ugly?"

"We're supposed to be focusing on your story." She waggled her finger his direction, refusing to give him the compliment he was obviously fishing for.

He nodded, though a smirk hovered around his lips. "Right. It turned out that baseball was something I did pretty well. They put me in as a pitcher, and I helped the team go to state my sophomore year of high school."

"Wow."

"Yeah. I used to be able to throw a pitch around ninety miles an hour." He motioned with his arm in a circle like he was throwing a curveball.

"Good grief!"

"Then the Robertses really started trying to adopt me instead of just fostering. They'd always had that in mind as a possibility, but the state was taking longer than we wanted, so they went in and tried to expedite the process. Instead, it made my birth mom aware of me and where I was. She'd evidently been in counseling for several years and suddenly realized she needed to find me."

"So you got to be reunited with your mom?" She sat back in her chair. Something warned her that while this sounded like it was headed for a happy ending, it might not be the way she expected. After all, he had the name of his foster parents. Surely that was no coincidence.

He shook his head. "I met with her, but only when they agreed Mrs. Roberts could go with me. She'd been more of a mother to me than anyone else in the world. We agreed before the meeting that I would try to give her a real chance to talk to me, not to go in with any preconceived judgments, but it was so hard. How does a sixteen-year-old boy go in without some hurt and face a woman who gave him up when he was a baby?"

Reaching over, she placed her hand on top of his.

His gaze met hers, and he smiled. "She didn't want me back

to raise me. I think she knew she'd missed her chance. But she wanted to ask my forgiveness, to make sure I was okay."

He squeezed her fingers and clasped them between his instead of letting go. They sat for a few moments, listening to others walking through the parking lot, to some crickets chirping nearby, to the door jingle as it opened and closed.

"Anyway, she agreed to sign over her rights and let the Robertses adopt me after that. At first, I was still a little unsure about it." He gave a little shrug. "After all, what if they changed their minds? I mean, I was almost seventeen, nearly an adult. Was it worth it to put myself through that kind of buildup if I might be let down?"

The quiet stretched for so long she had to prompt him for more. "But you obviously did. Your last name is Roberts now."

He nodded. "Yes. The Robertses had proven to me again and again and again how much they cared. They were at every ballgame, even the ones in other towns. They bragged about me to their friends as my grades rose in school. She made sure she had chocolate chip cookies for me at least a couple times a month, and she made a huge deal out of birthdays and Christmas."

A chuckle shook his shoulders. "I was pretty proud of being able to sign my name 'Grayson Roberts' after that court date. They surprised me by ordering a new letterman jacket with my new last name. My former name was Chadwick. It threw the college recruiters for a loop for at least a month, but they caught up with me again just in time to offer me a great scholarship."

"Which you used to get a degree in computer technology." She intertwined her fingers within his. "Right?"

"Right."

"That's an amazing story, Gray." She pulled her hands free. "Do they live in the area?"

"You saw the song leader at church tonight?"

She jerked her head up. "Really? That was him? Oh."

He chuckled. "You're remembering how dark his skin is compared to mine, aren't you?"

"It definitely wasn't what I was expecting." She shook her finger at him. "You didn't introduce me."

"I had texted them earlier to let them know you were coming but that I didn't want to scare you off, to sort of just keep it on the down-low. I wouldn't have minded them coming and meeting you, but evidently, they decided I meant for them to stay back until I said otherwise."

"They know about me?"

"Yeah." His lips stretched into a sheepish grin. "You've been one of my favorite topics of conversation lately. They've actually been praying for you."

Adrian pressed a hand to her temple. "All this time, you let me go on and on about how awful my life was when I was growing up, how you wouldn't understand, when in reality, you didn't have a home either."

"I did have a home, though. I just had to find it."

She shook her head. "Or, rather, it found you. The Robertses."

"No." He leaned forward to catch her eyes.

She frowned. "What?"

"The Robertses gave me a home, yes. But it's not my real home."

"Okay. Yeah." She lifted one shoulder. "You have a different home now, probably, but you know what I mean."

"No." He took her hands again. "I mean I found my home when I found God."

She ducked her head. *Here it comes.*

"Anyway, I just wanted you to know more about me. You seemed to think I'd had a perfect childhood. It wasn't. I'm not comparing it to yours. Your hurt is real, and everything you had to go through is real, too. But I will say I can understand the feeling of being displaced, of everyone looking at you like you're different, of wishing for a home."

Glancing back up, she met his stare. He had some of the prettiest, purest blue eyes she'd ever seen. Now his gaze was complete sincerity.

"Maybe we can work through it together," he whispered.

And back down at the table went her focus, as she swallowed back a lump in her throat. "I don't know what you're expecting from me. I'm not sure I can be the girl you think I am."

"Because I'm so perfect?"

"You might as well be." She pulled her hands away again and waved them through the air. "Look at you. Look at the way you've come back from everything that happened to you in the past. And I'm sitting here wallowing in my misery, refusing to get past it, refusing to forgive." A tear escaped and traced its way down her cheek.

He moved from the chair across the table to the one next to her and laid a hand on her shoulder. "Trust me when I say I'm not perfect. But maybe together, we can strive for perfection and can work towards getting you past your misery and help you forgive. Because the fact that you just said you hadn't shows me you know you probably need to."

She brushed madly at the tears now flowing more freely down her face. "Gray, I'm such a mess."

"Have you seen my desk? I like messes!"

A laugh burst from her, and a huge weight seemed to lift from her chest. He helped her stand and pulled her into a hug. The scent of his cologne filled her senses, and his arms brought comfort and a sense of rightness.

"I'll still have to leave soon." Her voice was quiet as she pulled away to look at him.

"Trust God, and trust me, okay?"

"What if I can't?"

He placed a finger on her lips. "Try."

She found herself nodding despite the doubt that lingered in her heart. *What am I getting myself into? Why does it seem like as much as I've figured out this weekend, I still have so much further to go?*

20

Adrian stared at the ceiling of her hotel room as she lay in bed that night. Gray had given her much to think about, on top of what Dad and Danielle had already stirred up. She'd been fighting for so long. She'd distanced herself from God—or at least tried to—just like the bulletin board at the church building in Sassafras said. He didn't move, and He didn't change, but she'd believed He was something different from what He was.

Not necessarily a grandpa like in the sermon tonight, though. Her eyes followed the beam of a car as it drove past. But someone who wasn't loving either. *Or maybe I just don't understand love. Is that it? How can I be in a relationship with Gray if I don't know what love is? How can I go back to trying to be a Christian if I don't know what love is?* The Bible says a Christian should be known by her love.

She got up and padded across the room, using only the dim glow of the streetlight outside to find her duffel bag she hadn't completely unpacked. Earlier, she'd discovered a package from her mom but hadn't taken the time to open it. Now she pulled it out and carried it to the living room. Clicking on a lamp, she fingered the plain paper covering whatever her mother wanted her to find.

"Something tells me you might be ready to have this back." Her mom's handwriting hadn't changed in all the years she'd known her. It looped and curved across the page in a graceful script.

Adrian pulled back the paper and removed a book as familiar to her as anything else she owned. Her parents had given her this Bible when she was ten, something to take with her to summer camp. The splotch of paint on the back remained from where she'd set it down on a craft project before allowing it to dry completely. She opened the front to the first page.

"Lovingly given to Adrian Diane Stewart the summer of her tenth year of life, from her parents, James and Caroline Stewart. May you always use this to find your way in life, to ground you, protect you, and guide you. We love you."

She ran her fingers over the words. Her sister had one almost identical, except the cover was pink instead of blue—each girl got her favorite color—and was made out to Danielle Alyson Stewart. Flipping through the pages, she noticed passages she'd highlighted in high school, words she'd underlined, and notes made in the margins.

How did I get from marking up my Bible and using it enough the maps are falling out of the back, to leaving it at my parents' and not missing it for over four years?

Her eyes caught on a passage in 1 John 4 that was marked in pink. "He who does not love does not know God, for God is love. In this the love of God was manifested toward us, that God has sent His only begotten Son into the world, that we might live through Him. In this is love, not that we loved God, but that He loved us and sent His Son to be the propitiation for our sins. Beloved, if God so loved us, we also ought to love one another."

Well, I asked what love is. There you go. God loved me so much He gave up His son. Now I have to love others because of it.

She skimmed through the verse again. "He who does not love, does not know God." *But I do know God. It's not that I don't love people. I just don't trust them because they didn't love me.* She shook her head. It sounded ridiculous. Despite not opening her Bible in four years, she remembered she was supposed to forgive again and again—and, in the worst-case scenario, even supposed to love her enemies.

Is Dad right? *Am I just as bad as I think everyone else is? I was definitely wrong in what I assumed about Gray.* Could it be the same with all the others too? She took a deep breath and let her head fall to rest on the back of the couch.

"Are you there, God?" She whispered. "So many people want me to find my way back to You, but I don't know if I can. I'm having some major trust issues here, and I need Your help."

"GOOD MORNING." Gray gave her one of his sunny smiles from his normal spot in front of his computer.

She couldn't help but grin in return. She wasn't a morning person, but if she had to see someone first thing in the morning, he was the one she wanted to see. Wait. Had she just admitted she did want a relationship with him? She ducked her head and moved to her table.

"You okay?" He turned to look at her.

"Yeah." She pulled her laptop out of her bag. "Just thinking about a lot of things."

He nodded. "I'm here if you need to talk anything through."

"Thanks, Gray. We have a meeting this morning, right? Touching base to make sure we're where we need to be and discussing any last problems that require my attention?" She pulled up her email.

"Right. Want some coffee before we head upstairs?" He pushed back from his desk.

"Definitely. The cup I had at home won't cut it today." She

deleted a few messages and then stood next to him. Gazing up into his eyes, she caught her breath. Of course they'd been seated close together, but standing put them even nearer because he was only a couple inches away. The butterflies from the first few days she'd worked here were back, and from the flutters going on in her middle, caffeine must make them multiply.

"Hi," he whispered.

She ducked her head again and turned quickly away from him, trying to control the frenzy inside. Work. They were at work. Time to be professional. "So about that coffee ..."

Maybe her cheeks weren't quite as pink as they felt. As if she had that kind of luck. As she walked down the hallway to the kitchenette, she took a deep breath. And then another. He didn't say anything as they stood side by side and fixed their coffee.

Diane stuck her head in the doorway. "You guys coming?"

"On our way." Gray's voice sounded completely normal. Adrian hoped hers would be the same when she used it again too.

Around the conference table were Diane and Maggie, as well as several office managers and vice presidents of the company. This would more than likely be the last meeting Adrian attended here. She swallowed a lump in her throat at the thought of leaving soon. Only a few days more. Gray punched a button on the phone in the middle of the table and welcomed Brad to the conference.

"Good morning." Brad's familiar voice came through the line. "I understand we had some problems over the weekend."

"The reports didn't run correctly." Diane leaned forward when she spoke as if she needed to be closer to the device to be heard.

Adrian tapped her pen against the notepad in front of her. "We worked with Jorge and Dan yesterday so they could cut paychecks, but I'll continue working on the problem this week just to make sure it won't happen again."

"Okay. Everything else looking good?" Brad asked.

Several people around the room chimed in. Adrian marked down a few items mentioned that she could tweak. Mentally she calculated how much time the list would take her and wished for a few more items to add. Didn't these people realize her staying here depended on them?

"Great. Adrian, I'm sure you've been taking notes. Think you can get all that hammered out by the end of the week?" Brad asked.

Adrian swallowed a knot of disappointment. "Shouldn't be a problem. The biggest issue I'll be working on will be the payroll reports. I'll be in touch later today about those."

"Perfect. I'll talk to you then. Everyone else, it's been great. Call us as you need us. Adrian's there through the end of the week, and then you have access to help through our eight-hundred number or via our online chat." Brad ended the call, and the meeting broke up as employees headed to their offices. A few shook Adrian's hand as they walked past her.

"We're going to be sad to see you go, Adrian." Vice President Riley said as she gathered her papers. "You've been a huge asset to this company. And I hate trying to fix things over the phone and online."

Adrian laughed and nodded. "It's nice to have someone there to fix it in person, isn't it?"

"Definitely. Wish we could keep you." Riley nodded as she walked by.

And for the first time in forever, Adrian rather wished she could stay.

"Would you like to do lunch today?" Gray walked beside her back to the dungeon—a place Adrian had come to consider something much more pleasant.

"Maybe. Let me see what I can do with these numbers I printed off yesterday, see what caused them not to match up correctly." She waited until he moved to his seat before reclaiming hers.

"Sure. And I'm right here if you think another set of eyes might help."

She glanced over her shoulder at him. "Thanks."

Several hours later, she threw her pencil down in frustration. That was the third time she'd added up the columns of the test report she'd run and got a completely different answer each time. Gray's cologne rolled over her, and his hand covered hers before she could reach out to pick her pencil up again.

"How about a break? Maybe some lunch will help clear your head and make it easier when you come back." He leaned down so he could look into her eyes.

She rolled her shoulders to work out some of the tension. "Okay. Maybe a break will help. But not too long."

"Cross my heart." His finger drew an *X* over his chest. "I won't make you leave the office for more than an hour, tops."

A grin stretched her lips of its own volition.

GRAY TOOK her back to the barbeque place where he'd first treated her to lunch all those weeks ago.

A dribble of sauce trailed down her chin, and she swiped at it. "I'm going to miss this."

"The barbeque or lunch with me?" Gray popped a French fry in his mouth.

"Both. Probably the second one more than the first. I'm not used to getting barbeque like this." She pulled off a piece of sandwich and chewed it thoughtfully.

She'd miss him more than barbeque. He'd take it. Especially considering it meant she'd done almost a one-eighty since Thursday night when she didn't want a relationship.

"St. Louis isn't that far." Gray played with the straw in his cup.

"Four and a half hours. Much too far to come for a sandwich." She put down the forkful of beans.

"I could come up there, and we could take in a baseball game." He nudged her foot with his.

"What if I'm off in another state training someone?" Adrian picked apart a fry on her plate.

"Then you might be even closer. You don't know what your next assignment is yet, do you?"

"No." She shook her head, then frowned. "And that's really odd too. Usually, Brad has me looking into a new company several weeks before I'm finished with my current job. This time, he hasn't even mentioned one. Maybe I'll get a little break between gigs."

"Then you could spend some more time with your family. You don't get to see them much, right?"

"Yeah. More in the last few months than the last few years, honestly." She picked at some crumbs on the table. "And I need to go back and go to church with them soon. I think I'm almost ready."

Reaching across the table, Gray grabbed her hands. "Could I go with you?"

"So you can see me humiliate myself by going forward and asking forgiveness?" She raised an eyebrow.

He shook his head. "So I can support you as you humble yourself to God's will."

"I still don't know how I'll be able to trust people. Or God." She started to pull her hands from his, but he held on.

"Trust takes time. It has to be earned. But it can't be earned if you never even let them try." He squeezed her fingers. "Do you trust me?"

She looked up into his eyes as he searched hers. "Yes. And it terrifies me. Especially with me leaving soon. What if—"

"No *what if*s." He tapped his fingers against hers. "We'll take things one day at a time. Okay?"

She locked eyes with him, held on to his hands a little tighter. "Okay."

"Together. You're not alone in this. I'm here. God's here. No matter what happens, we'll be okay. If I could survive being given up and passed around as a kid, and you could survive moving and starting over again and again growing up, we can do anything now, right?"

A laugh burst from her lips. "Sure. Why not?"

"Just remember Philippians 4:13."

"I can do all things through Christ who strengthens me." She quoted.

"Hold on to that. It's true." He motioned to her plate. "You ready to head back to the office?"

"Ugh. Let me eat a few more bites."

He grinned and slowly released her fingers. "Sure."

On the way back to the office, she stared out the window. "It's strange."

"What? Memphis?"

She laughed. "No. Just thinking about the fact that I grew up in the church and you didn't, but your faith is greater than mine. Isn't that odd? You went through so much more than I did, but you readily accepted God when you found him. I knew God my whole life and rejected him when I left home."

"First of all, let's not compare what we went through." Gray turned into the parking lot. "Second of all, it took me a while to accept God. My mom and dad were great, and they were very patient with me. But it took several years of them teaching and taking me to church services and showing Christian love before I actually believed it was real." He turned to face her.

"Thirdly, you're finding your way back to God, and that will probably make your faith a lot stronger than it was. All that matters is you're trying."

"Thanks, Gray. You know, Danielle said if God wanted me back, He'd find a way to get me there. I'm not sure any of this would have happened if I hadn't met you."

He grinned. "I'm honored to be used by our God. But I'm glad he let me meet you no matter the reason." Leaning forward, he dropped a kiss on her cheek.

"I guess I better get inside." She glanced at her watch. "Brad wanted to talk around two this afternoon, and it's already after one."

"Does it bother you that I kissed you?" Gray asked before she could get out.

She stared in the direction of people walking into the office. "I don't know. I'm still new to this whole relationship thing. I'm still learning, okay? Be patient with me?"

Be patient with her. Of all the Christian virtues he struggled with, patience was probably the worst. But she was worth it. No argument there.

"You bet. Of course, I have to say you're the first girl I ever kissed and had fireworks go off."

She rolled her eyes. "Wow. With a line like that, I'm surprised I'm not the first girl you ever kissed."

"You don't like my pick-up lines?" He pouted a bit before chuckling.

His hand found its place at the small of her back as they wove their way through the office and down to the basement again. She sat down to her email while he checked his. As she dialed Brad, he slipped out to check on the rest of the IT staff.

If only he had a way to keep her here. Would that allow her to relax and go all-in on a relationship with him? Just one hurdle, but it was a huge one.

21

"Will it be an easy fix?" Brad asked on speaker phone.

She ran her pencil down the rows of numbers. "I'm not sure. Every time I think I've figured it out, something else doesn't add up. I've got Jorge working with the payroll company, too. We're thinking our programs aren't communicating correctly."

"Well, do as much as you can this week, but go ahead and come home Monday. You've got Healthcare for All set up to go now, and they can do the rest through our IT department over the phone or chat."

Home. Adrian still wasn't sure what that word meant, but she no longer thought of St. Louis as home. Maybe the warm feelings she had toward the city were simply because of the movie she'd loved for so long. But her heart rebelled against the thought of leaving Memphis now. Did that make it home?

"Go ahead and tell her now. It's no use prolonging the inevitable." Michael's voice came softly over the line from St. Louis. He didn't normally join in on their phone conversations because he was more the tech brains of their company while Brad covered customer relations.

"What's up?" Adrian paused in what she'd been doing to

focus more on the phone call. Was she about to get the promotion she'd been working toward the last few years?

Brad let out a sigh. "There's really no easy way to tell you this, Adrian. You've been such a great member of our company for almost five years now. You were a major part of building this software and have been one of our top trainers."

"Tha-anks." Adrian wasn't sure how to take the compliments after the way Brad started them. Tell her what?

"Some of the state governments have been redoing the way their in-home healthcare companies are required to report their time. Our program no longer meets all of their specifications in four of the states we're in."

"Woah." Adrian reached out to steady herself even though she was already sitting down. "That's huge. So what will it take to update our software to meet their requirements?"

Another long sigh came from Brad's end. "It's not that simple. Trust me. Michael and I have run all the numbers and can't come up with a way to bounce back easily from this. That takes out over half of our clientele in the next three months. It's a huge hit to our company."

Adrian blinked. "So, what are we going to do?"

There was a pause on the other end. "We're having to let some people go."

A stone formed in the pit of Adrian's stomach, messing with the pork she'd enjoyed at lunch. Was he saying what she thought he was?

"With so few states in our surrounding area able to use our software right now, we don't need your position at this time."

Was the room spinning? Adrian placed a hand on her head to try to make it work again. Why couldn't she get a full breath?

"Adrian? Are you still there?" Brad asked.

"Yes." It came out a whisper. She cleared her throat and tried again. "Yes. I'm here." It was still quiet but loud enough to hear.

"I'm so sorry, Adrian. If there were anything we could do differently, we would. We're trying to figure things out still.

Trying not to have to close the whole company. We don't want to let the few businesses who can still use our software down, but this is a huge blow to our numbers.

"We'll still cover your costs for this month, and we'll pay you all the vacation time you've got saved up. I know it's not much, but the way you've been working, it will give you a couple more months to find something else. And you will. Because you're a great worker. And we'll write that in the recommendation letter. I know someone will jump at hiring you."

"Thanks, Brad." Adrian tightened her lips to keep them from trembling. "I guess I'll swing by with the company computer next week."

"I'm really sorry, Adrian. I wish there were another way."

"Sure." Adrian swiped at a tear that escaped unbidden. "I'll be in touch, okay?" She was losing her ability to keep her voice steady. This phone call needed to end soon.

"Okay. Talk to you later."

She couldn't hit *end* fast enough. More tears streamed down her face. What would she do? She dashed at her cheeks to try and stem the flow, but they wouldn't stop. Of all the unprofessional things she'd done on this training job, this was probably the most unprofessional—that and falling for her coworker. Good grief! Gray couldn't see her like this!

She grabbed a tissue from her bag and dabbed at her face again, then jumped up to rush to the bathroom with as few people as possible seeing her. Right before she got to the door of the office, Gray appeared in it. She ducked her head and tried to squeeze past him, but he caught her and held her firmly.

"What's wrong? What's happened? Is it your dad again?"

Unable to talk, she shook her head. He gently pushed her back into the office and nudged the door mostly closed. She allowed him to walk her back to her chair. Sitting next to her, he pulled her to him, stroking her hair, rubbing her back.

Slowly the tightness in her chest eased some. A stone still lodged somewhere near her heart, but she could breathe a bit easier. She pushed away and dabbed the now-mostly-damp tissue across her cheeks again. No telling how splotchy her face looked, how swollen her eyes probably were.

"Can you talk now?" Gray leaned forward and lifted her chin so she'd look at him.

"I think so." She hiccupped and covered her mouth.

He grinned. "What happened?"

"I lost my job."

His grin turned quickly to a frown. "What? Did they fire you?"

"Yes." She shook her head. "No. I guess it's more like they laid me off. They're losing over half the companies that use their software. Several state governments are changing the way time has to be reported again—including four of the states using our program."

"Wow." He sat back, and she noticed her tears had left a wet spot on his shirt.

"Yeah. Is your company having to change software again so soon after switching to this one?"

"No. I would definitely know about it if we were. I mean, we would've known in time to not go with this company if the change were coming that quickly."

"Brad said in the next few months. Basically, this is my last week." Adrian slumped, her hands between her knees. "Gray, what am I going to do? This is the only job I've ever had."

"You're so smart, Adie. I'm sure you'll find a job again like that." He snapped his fingers.

"I was one of the three people who wrote this software. I thought I'd be promoted soon." Adrian shook her head. "Is God testing me? I told him I'd try to trust Him, and then this happens?"

"Adrian—"

She stood and walked to the door. "I need to go splash water on my face. I'll be back."

Taking her time in the bathroom, she thought about

everything that had happened, wondering what she should do, not sure how to face Gray. The cold water helped diminish the splotches on her cheeks, anyway. She finger-combed her hair and pulled it back into a ponytail. Taking a deep breath, she straightened her shoulders. She was a professional. The first thing she'd do was finish this job.

Gray wasn't in the office when she got back, but he'd left her a cup of coffee and a note that he'd been called into another meeting. She took a sip and smiled as she realized he'd learned how she liked it over the last few months. She grabbed the reports and started adding again. If nothing else, she had to fix this problem before the end of the week.

DIANE WAS ALSO in Vice President Riley's office when Gray arrived. "You wanted to see me?"

"Come on in." Riley flipped through some reports while Gray slid into the chair next to Diane. "I wanted to go over some of these issues from last weekend. See how things were going to make sure they don't happen again."

"Adrian has assured me she should be able to get it worked out this week between what she's doing on our end and what they're doing in St. Louis." Diane clasped a planner in her lap. Why she carried the thing, Gray had no idea. There wasn't any room left on it to scratch a note.

Gray would chime in but wasn't sure what to say. Half his mind was back with Adrian, hoping she was okay, wishing he were there to keep comforting her. But he also knew no matter what happened after this week, she'd pull herself together enough to be able to finish making those reports work. He'd seen her work ethic get her through several rough days now.

"Good." Riley nodded.

"Gray and I have discussed how nice it would be to have someone here like Adrian all the time." Diane leaned forward a bit in her seat. "Someone who knew the software and could free up some of the IT guys to handle the other problems like servers and phone stuff."

"Okay. Give me more." Riley sat back and tapped a finger to her chin. "Sell me on this. I'm not making any promises, though, because the last time I checked our budget, there was no room for a new position."

His heart did a loop-de-loop. *Are you really going to make it so easy, God?*

"No offense to Gray." Diane glanced over at him. "But he couldn't have fixed the problem over the weekend the way Adrian did, even with the online chat. He's great at his job, but he didn't always know where to look for things automatically like Adrian did. Without her, payroll would've been late."

"But you said she's fixing the problem now, so this shouldn't be something you have to face each week, right?" Riley raised an eyebrow.

Gray swallowed a groan. Time to find more perks. "You said we might have to switch payroll software too, right? Will that be soon?"

"Yes, but it wouldn't be the same as what Adrian's been working with."

"Right, but it would still have to sync with the MidUSLogIn software. Which means you could run into this or something similar again. Possibly even more problems if they aren't able to get it all fixed in the first run-through."

"That's still probably only a few months." Riley tapped a finger to the calendar on her desk. "Not full-time."

"Plus, any time you have to hire a new coordinator, you'd have to train them." Gray ticked the points off on his fingers. "And any time one of the attendants out in the field tries to clock in wrong, it has to be cleaned up. And because she has knowledge on more than just the MidUSLogIn software and can easily figure out others, she could help in other areas too."

Gray pulled from the recesses of his mind all the ideas he

could. "And I know how much both you and Diane detest trying to work with someone over the phone or a chat screen. Having someone like Adrian would eliminate the need for that."

"You're certain we'd need her for longer than a few more months?" Riley raised a brow. "Assuming she'd even be available."

Should he let slip what he knew? Maybe it would add just enough to tip this to his favor. "She's actually being let go. The company is downsizing right now, and she found out this afternoon that her position is being cut."

Diane gasped. "That's awful."

"Okay." Riley nodded. "Let me get with the others and see what we can work out. If she's a free agent, I'd definitely love to keep her talents nearby. But I'm still not sure if our budget will allow it. Do you know how long she has?"

"She finishes here this week and then has a bit of vacation pay coming to her. Several weeks, I think." Gray's throat was tight with the possibilities.

"Don't mention this to her yet. I don't want to get her hopes up only to have them crushed when we can't make it work." Riley glanced between the two of them.

"Thanks for at least trying." Diane stood. "It would be such a relief to know I had someone like her I could run to in an emergency."

"Okay." Riley nodded and waved at them, an obvious dismissal.

Gray was jittery. The situation looked so much brighter now, and he couldn't even share the hope with Adrian. But he could pray for God to help Riley find the money. And he could offer support in other ways.

THERE WAS no sign of Gray making it back to their shared space by the time Adrian was ready to leave that evening. Reluctantly she packed her bag and headed to her hotel. She'd hoped to see him again, have him remind her she'd be okay. Maybe she'd believe it better coming from him.

A knock at her door interrupted her debate on whether to heat up a frozen dinner or run out to grab a sandwich. She peeked through the peephole and saw Gray. She grimaced. Her ratty old blue jeans with the holes in the knees and old high school T-shirt had seen much better days. When he knocked again, she knew she'd just have to let him see her at her worst.

She opened the door and lifted her eyebrows. "Hey."

"Oh, good. You're ready."

She frowned a little. "Ready for what?"

"A picnic. Let's go."

"Did I know we were going on a picnic?" She searched her brain to see if maybe she'd forgotten something.

"Um. Probably not. I just thought it might do you some good. We can go up to Shelby Farms and see the buffalo, walk around the lake, eat the sub sandwiches I picked up. Too much?" He rocked back on his heels and stuck his hands in his pockets.

She couldn't help but grin. "Buffalo?" She grabbed her purse and locked the door behind her.

"Yeah. There's a sort of ranch they live on. Mostly you can just see them as you drive up." He opened the car door for her and then got in the other side.

He smoothly maneuvered through the evening traffic. Memphis rush hours weren't as bad as some places she'd been— like Chicago. But there were a lot of people in this city who thought the rules didn't apply to them. She counted two cars zooming through a traffic light after it turned red.

The buffalo were hard to miss as they drove into the park. Huge, hairy beasts eating grass in a fence across from the lake. She took it all in as they parked.

"Hungry?" He pulled a small cooler from behind his seat—the same one that held ice cream the week before—and they got out. A park bench next to the lake was empty, a perfect spot to eat dinner.

"It almost feels like I've been in Memphis forever, like this is the most natural thing in the world to be doing." She accepted the sandwich he offered.

"Maybe it should be." He took a bite off his own sub and stared out at the lake.

"So you think I should just try to get a job in Memphis?"

He shrugged and glanced at her. "There are worse places in the world to live."

She chewed a few moments. "If you're thinking I should move here to be close to you, I have to admit it's growing on me. But what if something happens and you change your mind about me? Then I'd be back to square one, living in a city with no friends."

"Or you could start going to church with me on a regular basis and let Victoria and Christine be friends with you. They ask about you all the time." He balled up his trash. "Not that I expect to change my mind."

"This is so hard, Gray." She tucked a leg under her as she turned to face him. "When I was very young, I remember thinking God would always take care of me, that I had nothing to worry about, that the church was made up of the best people. But it got harder and harder to believe as I grew up. I mean, the more we had to move and the more difficult it was to make friends, the worse my faith got.

"And I guess it's probably my fault because I didn't fight against it. I let it happen, didn't attend church services regularly in college, didn't take my Bible with me when I moved out, quit visiting my family on a regular basis so I wouldn't have to admit I wasn't who they wanted me to be."

He reached over and gently grasped her shoulder.

She stared out at the lake. "And now, when I finally decide that maybe it would be better if I went back, if I tried to trust God again, if I start believing that all people who claim to be Christians aren't intrinsically hypocrites and judges, then this happens." She threw her hands up in the air. "What am I supposed to think?"

Tearing off a piece of bread he had leftover, Gray tossed it to some ducks waddling by. "I was just starting to believe in God when my birth mother showed up."

Adrian gave him her full attention but didn't interrupt.

"I guess I thought she wanted me back. I had this image in my head of having this great life with my 'real' mom, of always being happy and her just gushing all over me, asking me to forgive her for abandoning me, saying she'd always regretted it and wanted to make it up to me for the rest of her life." He shook his head. "She did apologize and say she regretted how hard my life had been when I was younger. But she still didn't want me."

It was Adrian's turn to lay a comforting hand on his shoulder. He met her eyes, reached up, and squeezed her fingers. She could almost see in the depths of his eyes the sixteen-year-old boy hurt by his mother.

"I thought God was playing this awful, mean trick on me. Why would He bring my mom to me and then take her right back away?"

"But you love the Robertses, right?"

"I do now." He nodded. "And I think I was definitely in the beginning stages of love back then, too, but I hadn't had real love for so long—if at all—I didn't even know what it was. I didn't realize it was my dad being there for every baseball game, my mom making my favorite cookies to celebrate good grades, them taking me to church and making sure I attended every devotional and youth activity. I thought it could only come from the woman who actually bore me."

Adrian didn't know what to say. She'd been thinking about love, yes, but in reality, she did know what love was because her family had displayed it to her over and over and over again. They still were in their worry over her soul, in their reaching out every way they knew how, in regretting their own jobs because they thought it had taken her salvation away.

"I know better now, but back then, it hurt like crazy when I found out she wasn't going to take me with her. I'd been excited about the Robertses adopting me before we found out about her, but that put a damper on it for a while. Come to find out, she'd been living with a guy who was abusing her, she was addicted to drugs, and she didn't have any money. She knew I'd be better off staying where I was instead of coming with her."

"How did you find that out?" Adrian leaned forward.

"She didn't show up for one of her counseling sessions. The counselor was worried about her because he'd seen some bruises, so he went investigating. They pulled her out and took her to a halfway house, got her some help." He smiled at Adrian. "The Robertses explained the situation to me.

"They gave me the option of waiting to see if she'd get her life together or going ahead with the adoption. But later that week, she left the halfway house and went back to her boyfriend. She couldn't resist. I was furious. That's why I told the Robertses to go ahead with the paperwork. It was a stupid reason but brought about great results."

"You let them adopt you because you were mad at your mom?"

He laughed. "Imagine what would happen if teenagers everywhere could do that!"

She giggled along with him, enjoying some relief of tension.

"Anyway, all that to say, God works in mysterious ways. And everything that happens is not necessarily an act of God. Sometimes things just happen. We live in a fallen world. And yes, God allows men to make their own choices, which means, in a roundabout way, He does allow things to happen. But that doesn't make it His fault.

"If you let Him, He'll work it out for good." Gray wrapped an arm around her shoulder. "The Robertses worked out a way to do Bible studies with my mom a few years ago. She became a

Christian last year and has worked to get her life together. Now I have two moms."

"Your parents sound amazing."

"They are." He paused. "They'd like to meet you. Maybe I could take you over there for dinner later this week?"

"Um." Her heart skipped its rhythm. Dinner with his parents? Wasn't that practically saying they were engaged or something?

"You just said they sounded amazing. And I've met your family. It's only fair."

Why did his argument have to be so valid? "Fine. You win."

They put the cooler back in his car and then strolled hand in hand around the lake as the sky grew dimmer. Families rode by on bicycles, people rushed by with dogs, some walked quickly to the beat on their headphones. She and Gray just enjoyed the peace.

"I'm glad you trust me. I'll do my best not to let you down. I'm still only a human, but maybe with God's help, I can live up to most of your expectations." Gray pulled her close before they got back in the car.

"You're crazy. You exceeded my expectations from the first time I saw you." She accepted his quick kiss and then smiled at him. "You weren't the only one who was intrigued during that first video conference."

He gave her one of the sunniest smiles she'd ever seen from him. "Here's hoping I can keep it up, then."

Back at her hotel, he parked, squeezed her hand. "I'm praying hard for you. God has something great in mind, I'm sure. Don't let your worries about what is to come cloud your faith. You're a computer guru. Someone will be blessed to have you on their staff."

She took a deep breath. "Here's hoping. For the rest of the week, though, I've decided to just give my best to the job I still have. I know it won't change their minds. But I can't abandon you guys either. You deserve my best."

"With an attitude like that, this week will go by much better than this afternoon did." He kissed her cheek and waved as she paused at the door of the hotel.

She walked back up to her room. *If Gray believes I can do this, then I can. Actually, I know I can do this. I'd already decided it before our talk tonight. He just helped confirm some things.*

She sent up a silent prayer. *Help me do this, God.*

22

Thursday afternoon, Gray joined in as Adrian hummed. She sheepishly glanced over at him, but he just grinned.

"What was I humming? I don't even really think about what song is running through my head, just let it come out in a hum." She clicked a few more times on the project she was completing and hit *save*.

"'Great is Thy Faithfulness.'" Gray typed a few words and then turned to face her. "One of my favorites."

She gave a little nod. "I've been thinking about the words a lot lately. I didn't believe them for a long time, but I'm beginning to see things differently. Even when I didn't want to admit it, God has taken care of me. He is much more faithful than I will ever be."

"So you quit worrying about the job situation?" Gray tilted his head as he studied her.

"Not completely. I mean, it's Thursday. My week's almost up. But I did get a call this morning." She closed her laptop and twisted to look at him. "Another company who has similar software and programs to MidUSLogIn Inc. They heard about the cutbacks and made me an offer. I'd basically be doing the same job I've been doing for Brad and Michael."

"Where are they based?" Gray leaned forward with his elbows on his knees. He still hadn't heard from Riley, so if this company was close, it could be even better.

She pursed her lips a moment. "Cincinnati."

His heart sank. "Ohio."

"That's the one."

He didn't know what to say. Ohio wasn't any closer than St. Louis had been. Maybe even farther.

"It's a sure deal, a good salary, nice benefits. And it's something I know how to do. I'll just have to be trained on how their software is set up, and then I can run with it." She splayed her hands out on her knees. "I haven't given them an answer yet. I asked them to give me a week to sort of finish up with MidUSLogIn and then see where things stand."

He nodded, trying to be supportive. "It sounds great, Adie. Like an answer to prayers."

She hummed a bit under her breath. "Yes and no. I've learned from my past that sometimes answers to prayers aren't always the obvious thing that comes up. My dad turned down several positions I thought might be great. He interviewed one time with a congregation somewhere in Georgia, really close to Atlanta. I was thinking about all the things we could do—go to Six Flags, see the aquarium, climb Stone Mountain.

"He saw how expensive it would be to live in that area, how large the schools were compared to what we were used to, how the church wasn't quite as sound as it should be. I was upset until I was older, and he told me his reasons. Then I could see while it looked good at first, it might not have been as great as my younger self thought it was. I need to view this offer from all angles. I wanted to ask for longer to decide but felt that would be unprofessional."

He gave her a smile not quite up to his usual warmth, but it was all he could muster. Monday afternoon Riley had given him hope. Now they were down to the deadline and nothing. He wasn't ready to let her go.

Focus. After all, God didn't need long to work things out. It could happen in less than twenty-four hours. Now whose faith was wavering?

Maybe a change in subject would help. "You still on for dinner tonight?"

"Yes." She wrinkled her nose. "Although I still can't believe I let you talk me into meeting your family."

"I've met yours." He jotted down a few notes on a sticky pad. "It's only fair."

"Okay." She finished packing up her laptop. "Let's get this over with."

He laughed and wrapped an arm around her shoulders as they walked down the hallway. "I'm not taking you to a firing squad. I'm taking you to meet the people who raised me ... and who want to meet you like you wouldn't believe."

NAOMI ROBERTS WAS petite with dark hair cut in a short bob and threaded through with silver. She pulled Adrian into a hug the moment the door was opened. Adrian was so caught off guard by the embrace, she just stood there and accepted it.

"I'm so glad to finally meet you. Gray has been talking about you all summer. We kept telling him he could bring you by, but he didn't want to scare you. As if we could be scary! Just drop your purse right there, and come on back to the kitchen with me." She didn't stop talking as she walked through the house, and Adrian scurried to follow her. She caught Gray laughing silently from where he watched and shot a dirty look his way.

"Mark! Guess who's here!" Naomi led her into a spacious kitchen from which all sorts of wonderful smells emanated.

Adrian recognized the man seated at the counter as the one who'd led singing last Sunday. She grinned, and he smiled in return. He probably wasn't as old as her dad, but his hair was starting to recede a bit, and he had reading glasses perched on his nose.

"Hi." Adrian shook his hand.

"Glad to meet you, Adrian. Naomi's been cooking all day, so we're all in for a treat." He folded the newspaper he'd been reading and set it aside.

"Hey, Dad." Gray hugged him and then sat on a barstool too.

"I wasn't sure what you'd like to eat, so I sort of fixed several different options, and we'll just have a smorgasbord." Naomi waved her hand at the dishes covering the counter. "You're not a vegetarian, are you?"

Adrian quickly reassured her. "No. I love meat."

Naomi pressed a hand to her chest. "Oh, good. I mean, not that we wouldn't like you just the same if you were. But I didn't want to offend you or anything."

"Mom, it's okay." Gray pulled Adrian a little closer to his side as if he could see she was wondering how to handle the situation. "She's going to love anything you make because you're a great cook."

Naomi dug through a drawer. "Well, let me stick spoons in everything and pour drinks, and we can eat."

They all held hands around the table as Mark led them in a prayer over plates laden with food. Adrian figured there was more food in this kitchen tonight than at a potluck dinner at church. She grasped Gray's fingers a little tighter, hoping she didn't disappoint his mom, who'd worked so hard to impress her.

Conversation flowed easily as Mark and Naomi took turns regaling her with funny stories about Gray's teenage years. "Don't forget the time he was sliding into second base and caught it wrong. His pants ripped right up the side, and you could see everything from his knee to his waistband."

"Mom!" Gray shot a dirty look across the table. "You should have seen the huge bruise I had for two weeks after. My whole leg was purple and green."

Adrian tried not to think about that mental image. For more reasons than one.

Gray's laughter filled the house a few minutes later as Mark divulged a prank Gray had been a part of during a church lock-in.

Leaning closer to Adrian, Naomi whispered, "Isn't that the best laugh you've ever heard? The first time I finally heard him laugh, I thought I'd found heaven. I swore that day to make sure I heard it again and again for the rest of my life."

"He's one of the happiest guys I've ever met." Adrian smiled and looked back and forth between Gray and his parents. "Even first thing in the morning." As her words replayed in her head, Adrian realized that sounded like she saw him earlier than arriving at work. Her cheeks heated, and she quickly added, "He's the most chipper guy in the office."

Naomi nodded. "It's hard to believe he was so angry and hurt when he first came to us. I'm still not sure how God brought about the miracle that changed him so completely, but I know it wasn't anything that Mark or I could do on our own."

"But you were definitely a big part of it. I'm so glad he found you." Adrian placed her hand on top of Naomi's.

"And we're glad he found you. As happy as he usually is, this summer has been different. When he talks about you, it's like he just lights up."

"What are you two whispering about over there?" Gray thumped the table.

"Just girl talk." Naomi pushed back and gathered her plate. "Who wants dessert?"

Despite thinking she wouldn't be able to take another bite after dinner, Adrian couldn't resist the banana pudding piled high with whipped cream. The coffee and company made it even sweeter. Hard as it was to imagine Gray bitter and angry, it was ridiculously easy to understand why he was so happy and grounded now.

Adrian leaned her head back against the car seat as they

drove back to her hotel that evening. Pictures ran through her head of what it must have been like to come to a house like that after not having a home for so long. It was like a piece of heaven on earth.

Gray glanced over at her. "Whatcha thinkin' about?"

"How lucky you are to have a home like that."

"Not lucky. Blessed. Blessed beyond measure." He parked in front of her hotel.

"I can't even imagine. Everyone asks me where home is for me. I'm never really sure what to tell them. I don't even know where I'd go if I wanted to go to a high school reunion next year. Danny says she's going to the one in Sassafras, but we were only there one year." Adrian fiddled with a loose thread on the bottom of her shirt. "What's the point of going to a homecoming if it's not really a place you think of as home?"

"What's your definition of home?" He reached over and took hold of her hand.

She shrugged. "I don't know. Someplace you've grown up, that you can have some roots, history, friends. Sort of like an anchor, I guess, to keep you grounded no matter how far away you move."

He was quiet for a moment, obviously thinking. "Have you ever heard the saying 'Bloom where you're planted?'"

"My mom has a sign saying that over her gardening shelves."

"I only got to talk to your mom for a few moments the day in the hospital, but I think she lives that saying better than anyone I've ever known." Gray squeezed her fingers. "It means wherever God puts you, make a life there. Thrive. Dig in and put down a few roots even if you have to transplant again later. It's worth it."

"But plants do better when they're not transplanted over and over again." Adrian shook her head. "We left so many gardens through the years. I always wondered why my mom bothered. She'd put all that work into it and just have to abandon it to someone else."

"But she enjoyed it, right?"

Adrian looked at him. "Yes."

"Then that's why. She determined for however long God let your family be there, she'd make it a home for you guys. I have a feeling home to her is wherever her family is. I know you've heard the saying, 'Home is where the heart is.'"

"Yes. I've also heard 'There's no place like home.' Are we just going to swap quotes?" She gave him a grin to show she was teasing a bit.

"No. But I think you see where I'm getting at. And if you add the verse in Matthew to the quote about home being where the heart is, I think you'll get a mental image of your mom."

He held up a finger in the air like he was reciting in a Sunday school class. "Do not lay up for yourselves treasures on earth, where moth and rust destroy and where thieves break in and steal; but lay up for yourselves treasures in heaven, where neither moth nor rust destroys and where thieves do not break in and steal."

"Okay. So my mom is okay with her home changing over and over again as long as she has her family ... and a garden. But what if I'm not?" Adrian pulled her hand free and laid it in her lap. "What if I can't be?"

"Did you think about the verse I just said? We have a home somewhere else."

She shook her head. "Heaven feels very far away. The thought of it doesn't take away the loneliness here on earth."

"That's what a church family is for." He rubbed his hand over her arm. "To help take away the loneliness, to have the support we need to get to heaven, our real home."

"And when you have to leave a church family behind?" Adrian blinked back moisture pooling behind her eyes.

"Then you find another one where you are. That's the wonderfulness of being a Christian. Wherever you go, there are going to be other Christians there too."

"What if they won't welcome me in? What if—"

He caught her chin in his hand. "There you go again with the *what if*s. Tell me truly, was it mostly just the teenagers who didn't let you fit in?"

Reluctantly she nodded her head.

"Try again with adults this time. Believe it or not, they tend to be friendlier." He ran his finger down the side of her face. "And if they're not, see if there's another congregation nearby that is. There are good people all over this world. You just have to find them."

She leaned into him, and his arms wrapped her up. She didn't want this evening to end because that would make it even closer to her last day of working here, her last day of knowing what she was supposed to do and with whom she'd be. She let the scent of his cologne fill her head, the steady beat of his heart under her ear calm her nerves.

"Maybe God doesn't always give us a home like you're thinking of here on earth because He wants you to have that anchor in heaven, to keep you grounded where you're headed instead of where you are." He whispered the words into her hair.

"What am I going to do without you nearby all the time?" She sat back and looked at him.

"We'll cross that bridge when we get to it." He kissed her forehead.

"Gray, my last day is tomorrow!"

He put his finger over her lips. "So let's enjoy every minute we can, and then we'll figure out after that together, okay?"

She released a long breath. "Okay."

23

"Okay, Diane." Adrian stuck her head in Accounting before she headed to the basement. "Can you do me a favor and do a test run for payroll for this week's hours? I want to make sure it's looking right before I leave today."

"Sure. Give me an hour, and I'll bring it to you." Diane didn't even look up from whatever she was doing.

"Thanks." Adrian pushed away from the door and walked down the stairs. She paused outside Gray's office and took a moment to collect herself. This was her last time to get her *good morning* from him. She blinked a few times and then walked through.

"Good morning." Gray smiled at her like the world wasn't ending. How was he that cheerful at the beginning of every single day? "Do you have lots to do today?"

"Some. Probably not enough to keep me from thinking, but I'll find some way to stay busy." She unpacked her laptop for the last time and set it up on her table.

"Thinking's not always a bad thing. I was thinking that maybe I'd join you at your parents' this weekend. You said that's where you were headed, right? Would they mind?" He didn't look away from his computer screen as he asked.

She stared at him for a full minute before answering. "I'm sure they'd welcome you with open arms. Especially since I'm planning to go to church with them for the first time in years. And it's mostly thanks to you."

"And your nosy sister. And your father being honest after his heart attack." Gray glanced over at her and grinned. "And the good head on your shoulders."

"Yeah, yeah."

A CHAT WINDOW popped open on Gray's computer from Riley that afternoon. "Can you come to my office for a short meeting?"

His heart thumped extra hard. Was this it? Or would his hopes be completely dashed?

"I've got a meeting, evidently. She says it will be short, so hopefully I'll be here before you leave ..." He was going to say, 'for the day,' but if Riley didn't come through, it could be 'forever.'

His throat constricted, and he forced a grin around the desire to frown.

"Sure." She frowned at him as if worried. Or maybe she, too, was just hating that this would take away time they could be together.

He reached over and squeezed her arm, wishing he could do more. Then, grabbing a pen and some paper, he headed out the door. *God, please.* It was all he could muster, but it would be enough. God knew his heart.

"Okay, I know we're down to the wire, but I need your help." Riley wasted no time when he entered her office. "We've rearranged several things and quit supporting another project, and we've found the money to keep Adrian. But I need to come up with the right wording for the contract. Help me figure out exactly what we're calling her position and what we need to list as her required tasks."

Gray sank in the chair, his knees weak with relief. *Thank you, God!*

"Gray?" Riley looked up. "You okay?"

"Just very happy." Gray grinned and ducked his head.

"Ah. I'd wondered if you two were getting close. The rumor mill put your names together a lot lately, but I hadn't received confirmation. And it does explain why you were pushing so hard for this."

"Can you blame me?"

Riley chuckled. "No. Guess we better see about finding her an office space of her own, assuming she agrees to this. No need to strain a new relationship by shoving it into such a tight space."

Gray swallowed the disappointment in the thought of not having her right there at his elbow every day. But it was worth it to have her closer than Cincinnati, no matter what. Surely she'd accept the job offer. This was too good to be true.

The clock said four minutes until five when they finalized the last line. Riley hit *print,* and Gray ran to grab it off the printer and take it downstairs to Adrian. He should just make it in time.

As he rounded the corner to the printer room, a burning smell hit his nostrils. *No. Not now.* But four or five different lights flashed on the giant piece of equipment, and one of Diane's staff was opening and shutting every door she could find to try to make the stupid thing work again. Gray groaned and barely kept himself from hitting the wall.

New plan. Just tell her about the job, and then they could come back up to look at the paperwork together. Okay. That should work just as well.

Down the stairs his feet pounded. He crashed through the door and almost took out Stan as he ran down the hallway. His watch said two minutes after five. Surely she'd waited for him. It was her last day. She wouldn't leave without saying goodbye, right?

Wrong.

His office was empty. No sign of her presence left. Not even a scrap of paper or a pen remained on the table where she'd sat the last six weeks. The only piece of her still there was a very slight whiff of her perfume.

Maybe he could catch her in the parking lot.

Sprinting back up the stairs and through the maze, he pushed through the front door, and watched her car turn onto the road. "Seriously?"

Riley stood at her door as he trudged back through the office. "What happened?"

"The printer was jammed, and by the time I got down there again, she'd left."

"Do I need to call her?"

He could just leave it to Riley. After all, it wasn't his position to offer. But he'd wanted to see the look on her face when she realized she could stay.

"What would you think of me catching up with her and offering the position in person? Would it be okay if she told you by Monday?" He rocked on his heels a bit. A crazy idea was forming in his head, and he was itching to leave so he could pull it off.

"Fine with me. Have a great weekend, Gray," Riley smirked.

Gray stopped back by the copy room and found the paperwork that had started this whole mess. He quickly gathered his things from the office and turned out the lights. Now, what else did he need before he cornered her in a way no one else would understand?

IT'D JUST ABOUT KILLED Adrian to walk out of the office that afternoon without seeing Gray again. But it was harder to sit there with nothing left to do and not know when or if he'd be back. So she'd taken the coward's way out.

It was easier this way. She wouldn't have to worry about the awkwardness of goodbye, of not knowing if or when she'd ever see him again. Sure, he'd asked to go with her this weekend to see her family, but wouldn't that just prolong the agony?

So she'd gathered her things a minute before five and headed back through Memphis one more time to her hotel. She kicked off her shoes, pulled her hair into a ponytail, and grabbed the last pint of ice cream from the freezer. She could eat healthy tomorrow. Tonight was all about comfort.

"I'm trying to trust You, here, God, but none of this makes sense." She flopped on the couch. "Sure, I'm back on speaking terms with You, but why bring me here where I met this amazing guy if You're just going to lead me even farther away again?"

A tear trickled down her cheek, and she swiped it away angrily. No. She would not give in to misery. She'd just chalk this up as a learning experience and know better next time. If another company offered to let her work knee-to-knee with a handsome man, she'd spit in their eye and go somewhere else.

A spoonful of chocolate and caramel toasted that sentiment. Nothing went with misery better than ice cream. And the love she knew she'd be lavished with tomorrow when she headed to Sassafras.

A little before six, a knock sounded at her door. "What in the world?"

She paused the movie dancing across her screen, half afraid she knew who was on the other side. The other half of her hoped with all her heart she was right.

Sure enough, those mesmerizing blue eyes stared back at her through the peephole. No time to check her appearance in the mirror. He banged on the door again.

She swung it open, unsure what he'd say. The look on his face had her taking several steps back. Was he angry? Surely not. Not over something like her leaving without saying goodbye.

He braced his legs apart, pointed his finger right at her, and said loudly enough it echoed in the hallway, "I love you."

Giggles and tears bubbled up from inside and burst out together. She covered her mouth with both hands to try and keep from breaking into hysterics. It was the scene from the movie. The one they'd talked about, when he'd asked what she'd do if someone ever did it to her. But now he had. And she had no idea what to say.

"You left too soon." He'd stepped inside now and lowered his voice to a normal level.

"I left at five." Well, one minute before, but he didn't need to know that.

"But I had something very important to tell you and was on my way down as you were leaving. If you'd only waited a few more minutes, you would've known." He took a few more steps her way, and she had to force her feet not to back up.

"Please tell me you're not proposing." The ridiculous thought escaped before she could catch it, and her eyes widened.

He chuckled. "No. This proposal doesn't come from me."

"What?" Now she was really confused.

"Vice President Riley asked me to give this to you and see if you'd have any interest." He pulled a stack of papers from behind his back and thrust them her way.

Tentatively she took a step in his direction. What in the world? Skimming the words, realization dawned on her. A proposal to come on as an employee at Healthcare for All. To stay in Memphis. To be with Gray.

Part of her wanted to jump up and down. But a vicious side of her came out, wanting to get Gray back just a little for the crazy way he'd come in here.

She stood there, a hand on each hip. "You have a lot of nerve."

One of his eyebrows went up.

"Did you know she was going to offer me a job?"

The edges of his mouth twitched a bit where he was obviously trying not to smile. "I might've known it was a possibility."

"You've known this for however long," she shook her finger at him, "and let me go on and on about how I didn't know what to do, how each day was closer to my last, how I wasn't sure how we could be together if we lived so far apart? You let me consider taking a job in Cincinnati!"

Straightening, he closed the gap between them so they were only about a foot apart. "So will you say, 'Yes'?"

"I might have to think about it."

He frowned a bit. "Is the salary not enough?"

She shook her head. "This actually looks like they might pay me a little more than I'm making now."

"Then what's holding you back?"

"You."

He blinked.

"Do you really think it's a good idea to continue working together if we're dating? How many people have killed their relationship just by working together every day?"

The grin beamed full-force across his face this time. "Just think about how much fun it will be to go to lunch together almost every day. Not to mention having an office where I can hear you hum, and you can scoff at my messes."

"This says I'd get my own office, actually."

He gave her what she could only call a pouty face. "I forgot that part. So you're leaving me?"

"Trying to protect our relationship."

"So you're going to accept?"

Holding up a finger, she stepped around him to grab her phone. She scrolled down her call list until she found the number she was looking for and pressed *Call*. "Mr. Walker? Yes, this is Adrian Stewart. Yes, thank you. I'm fine. Listen, I just wanted to thank you for the job offer with your company, but I've had something else come up, so I won't be able to accept your position."

She stifled a giggle as Gray did a happy dance beside her. As soon as she hung up, he scooped her up and spun her around.

She buried her head in his shoulder and wrapped her arms around his neck to hold on as tightly as she could.

He loved her. And she could stay.

"So, we're giving this a try?" She asked when she caught her breath.

"Yes, please." He pulled her tightly to him and kissed her ever so sweetly. "I told you God would work it out."

"With a little help from you?"

"Like I said the other day, I'm glad to be used by God."

24

Adrian clasped her fingers together to keep them from trembling as Dad wrapped up his sermon on Sunday. Gray reached over and gave her hand a squeeze of support. Danny wrapped her arm around Adrian's shoulders from the other side. Taking a deep breath, she straightened her spine as they stood to sing at the end of the sermon. It was time.

Woodenly she took a step out into the aisle and made the short walk up to the front of the auditorium. Dad ensconced her in an embrace as the congregation sang behind them. She handed him the piece of paper she'd written on earlier that morning and sat on the front row. Gray joined her a moment later, knowing she'd need his support.

Dad cleared his throat as he stood in front of everyone once they were all seated again. "This morning." He gave a slight cough. "This morning, my daughter, Adrian, has come forward to ask for forgiveness."

Holding up the letter, he read what she'd written. "For the last almost five years, I've allowed my feelings of hurt and pride to come between God and me. I decided I couldn't trust anyone in the church, despite not knowing them, based on the actions of others in my past. I come asking for forgiveness from you, the church family who has shown me nothing but love, and from God, as I try to build my faith up again, and come back to church."

Dad looked out at everyone in the auditorium and then at Adrian. "This is a day we've all been praying for. Thank you for being brave enough to admit this and for being humble enough to ask for help."

He led them in a prayer on her behalf, and the sense of peace that had been forming in Adrian over the last week grew even more. At the end of the worship service, Gray wrapped her in a tight hug, holding on maybe just a moment longer than was absolutely necessary. She didn't mind. Next in line was Dad.

"I'm so proud of you." He pulled her against him while tears ran down his cheeks. "I've always been proud of you, but never so much as at this moment."

Over Dad's shoulder, she saw most everyone in the congregation lined up waiting to shake her hand or hug her neck. In the past, this might have surprised her, but now she understood. Not everyone was like those she'd grown up with, and everyone deserved to be given a chance to prove they truly did embody Christ. These people did, and she welcomed their support this morning.

In the last week and a half, Adrian had told Gray she couldn't have a relationship with him, been reprimanded by her sister and counseled by her father, lost her job, and then come to find Gray, her family, and a job again. She still wasn't completely sure of her future. She'd drive to St. Louis tomorrow to finish her position with MidUSLogIn Inc., and find an apartment in Memphis to start over with Healthcare for All, later in the week. That was good enough for now.

And while so many things remained up in the air, she was willing to bloom where she was planted. For now, she planned to bloom in Memphis, and maybe, just maybe, she could make it a temporary home until she got to the real one—heaven.

Something told her that Grayson Roberts would help her in both journeys.

As they stepped into the sunshiny afternoon, he kissed her temple. Amazing how she'd gone from trying to avoid this guy to not being able to picture a future without him. For the first time in a long time, she remembered the true meaning of love.

AUTHOR'S NOTE

Hello dear readers,

Don't get me wrong. Not every preacher goes through what Adrian's father had to deal with in this story. But more often than not, ministers are held to a higher standard than others, and their families right along with them. They get used as a tool instead of a person, and I know of several instances where they're expected to do the work of several men. That being said, I'm blessed to have several preachers in my family.

This novel is very dear to me. I consider it my "what might have been" story. You see, Adrian chose to leave the faith and the church when Christians in her past let her down. She let her bitterness and hurt grow and fester to a point where she couldn't even see the good right in front of her because it wasn't what she expected. This could have been me.

A lot of the details in Adrian's history are similar to mine. We moved around a lot. I've still never lived anywhere longer than six years although my husband and I have great plans of settling for a while now. If I had allowed my past to color my future, I could have walked away from all I'd been brought up to believe.

However, thanks to some amazing people in my past, including my family and the ladies mentioned in my dedication, I was reminded over and over that God's way is always better even when it doesn't seem like it.

As I started writing this story and deciding what all to include, I knew I had to include *Meet Me in St. Louis*. As with Adrian, it's my favorite old musical. And, as with Adrian, it's the movie we watched the evening my dad announced to our family that we'd be moving the summer before my senior year of high school. Back then I wished my family could change their mind about moving just like the one in the movie. But it wasn't our choice—and God showed me later that it was really a good thing for all of us.

More often than not, I can look back and count my blessings for how I was raised. I had a great foundation for my own faith when I left home. I had the ability to make friends easily because I'd done it so many times. I knew how to be flexible, how to get established in a new place, and that the most important things after moving are finding a library and a church home—not necessarily in that order. And because of all of that, I was able to help my husband adjust through our various moves. He'd lived the same place most of his life.

If you're wondering about the job in this novel and how I knew so much about it, well, I worked for a home health agency for several years as the timekeeper. And during my short tenure there, I went through a situation like I included in this book, switching from one computer program to another. It was stressful but gave me much insight into what all to include in this story. Sometimes it's great to have worked so many different jobs.

I hope you've enjoyed Adrian and Gray's romance. It's a little different than some others I've written but one of the tales dearest to me too. If you did enjoy it, I'd love it if you'd leave a review. This helps other readers decide that the story is worth their time too.

Thanks so much for joining me. Until next time, God bless.
Amy

DISCUSSION QUESTIONS

1. Adrian thinks that if she doesn't allow herself to put down roots again, she'll never have to deal with the pain she suffered in the past. Do you think this really worked for her? Why or why not?

2. Adrian and Danielle both had disappointments and struggles in their past. What made Danielle come out with a strong faith while Adrian's wavered?

3. Adrian blames God for a lot of misery growing up. But so many of those struggles helped her become someone perfect for the job she has now. Have you ever looked back and seen where something you considered to be awful turned out to be a good thing down the road?

4. Adrian avoids her family because they make her feel guilty about no longer attending worship services. Do you think God gives us a sense of guilt when we're failing to do something we know is right?

5. Gray's past isn't perfect, and when Adrian finally finds that out, she can't figure out why he came out believing in God while she rebelled against Him. Have you ever wondered how people with a rougher past than yours have a stronger faith? Why do you think that is?

6. Gray has sworn he'll never date a non-Christian because of his birth mom and the troubles she had. Do you think this is a good choice? Why or why not?

7. Gray suggests to Adrian that she should consider blooming where she's planted. This isn't the easiest advice to follow but is often good. Have you ever had to find a way to thrive in a place you weren't happy in?

8. Adrian travels with her movie collection because she finds comfort in old musicals. What movies (or books or television shows) do you like to revisit? Do you have a movie connected to a memory, good or bad?

9. Do you identify more with Adrian or Danielle? Do you think Danielle has worked hard enough to understand Adrian's point of view?

10. Now that you've seen a sneak peek into some of the struggles some preachers' families have to deal with, what are some ways you can think of to make things better?

ABOUT THE AUTHOR

Multi-published author Amy R Anguish grew up a preacher's kid, and in spite of having lived in seven different states all south of the Mason-Dixon line, she's not a football fan. Currently she resides in Tennessee with her husband, children, and a bossy cat. Amy has an English degree from Freed-Hardeman University, which she intends to use to glorify God, and she wants her stories to show that while Christians face real struggles, it can still work out for good.

ALSO BY AMY R. ANGUISH

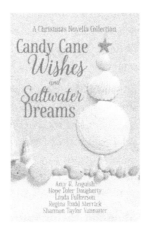

Candy Cane Wishes and Saltwater Dreams

A collection of Christmas beach romances

by five multi-published authors.

Mistletoe Make-believe **by Amy Anguish** – Charlie Hill's family thinks his daughter Hailey needs a mom–to the point they won't get off his back until he finds her one. Desperate to be free from their nagging, he asks a stranger to pretend she's his girlfriend during the holidays. When romance author Samantha Arwine takes a working vacation to St. Simon's Island over Christmas, she never dreamed she'd be involved in a real-life romance. Are the sparks between her and Charlie real? Or is her imagination over-acting ... again?

A Hatteras Surprise **by Hope Toler Dougherty** –Ginny Stowe spent years tending a childhood hurt that dictated her college study and work. Can time with an island visitor with ties to her past heal lingering wounds and lead her toward a happy Christmas ... and more? Ben Daniels intends to hire a new branch manager for a Hatteras Island bank, then hurry back to his promotion and Christmas in Charlotte.

Spending time with a beautiful local, however, might force him to adjust his sails.

A Pennie for Your Thoughts by **Linda Fulkerson** –When the Lakeshore Homeowner's Association threatens to condemn the cabin Pennie Vaughn inherited from her foster mother, her only hope of funding the needed repairs lies in winning a travel blog contest. Trouble is, Pennie never goes anywhere. Should she use the all-expenses paid Hawaiian vacation offered to her by her ex-fiancé? The trip that would have been their honeymoon?

Mr. Sandman by **Regina Rudd Merrick** – Events manager Taylor Fordham's happily-ever-after was snatched from her, and she's saying no to romance and Christmas. When she meets two new friends—the cute new chef at Pilot Oaks and a contributor on a sci-fi fan fiction website who enjoys debate—her resolve begins to waver. Just when she thinks she can loosen her grip on thoughts of love, a crisis pulls her back. There's no way she's going to risk her heart again.

Coastal Christmas by **Shannon Taylor Vannatter** – Lark Pendleton is banking on a high-society wedding to make her grandparent's inn at Surfside Beach, Texas the venue to attract buyers. Tasked with sprucing up the inn, she hires Jace Wilder, whose heart she once broke. When the bride and groom turn out to be Lark's high school nemesis and ex-boyfriend, she and Jace embark on a pretend romance to save the wedding. But when real feelings emerge, can they overcome past hurts?

Get your copy here:

https://scrivenings.link/candycanewishes

Saving Grace

Michelle Wilson's one goal in life was to become a top journalist at the local paper back in her hometown of Cedar Springs, AR. But on the way to bringing that dream to reality, a life-changing wreck interrupts Michelle's plans and adds an orphaned baby into the mix. Now, she has tough decisions ahead—did God put her in that accident to save baby Grace? And if so, why is it so hard to convince everyone else she should be the baby's new mommy?

Greg Marshall has been Michelle's best friend his whole life. He's thrilled she's moving back home, but not so sure about her sudden desire to be a single mom. His feelings for her have grown through the years, but she's never seemed to notice. Can he help Michelle with the adoption and grow their relationship at the same time?

Get your copy here:

https://scrivenings.link/savinggrace

Faith and Hope

Hope needs more hope. Faith needs more faith. They both need a whole lot of love.

Two sisters. One summer. Multiple problems.

Younger sister Hope has lost her job, her car, and her boyfriend all in one day. Her well-laid plans for life have gone sideways, as has her hope in God.

Older sister Faith is finally getting her dream-come-true after years of struggles and prayers. But when her mom talks her into letting Hope move in for the summer, will the stress turn her dream into a nightmare? Is her faith in God strong enough to handle everything?

For two sisters who haven't gotten along in years, this summer together could be a disaster, or it could lead them to a closer relationship with each other and God. Can they overcome all life is throwing at them? Or is this going to destroy their relationship for good?

Get your copy here:

https://scrivenings.link/faithandhope

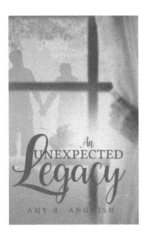

An Unexpected Legacy

When Chad Manning introduces himself to Jessica Garcia at her favorite smoothie shop, it's like he stepped out of one of her romance novels. But as she tentatively walks into a relationship with this man of her dreams, secrets from their past threaten to shatter their already fragile bond. Chad and Jessica must struggle to figure out if their relationship has a chance or if there is nothing between them but a love of smoothies.

Get your copy here:

https://scrivenings.link/anunexpectedlegacy

Scrivenings
PRESS
Quench your thirst for story.
www.ScriveningsPress.com

Stay up-to-date on your favorite books and authors with our free e-newsletters.

ScriveningsPress.com

MORE CONTEMPORARY FICTION FROM SCRIVENINGS PRESS

Perfectly Arranged by Liana George

Short on clients and money, professional organizer Nicki Mayfield is hanging up her label maker. That is until the eccentric socialite Katherine O'Connor offers Nicki one last job.

Working together, the pair discovers an unusual business card among Ms. O'Connor's family belongings that leads them on a journey to China. There the women embark on an adventure of faith and self-discovery as they uncover secrets, truths, and ultimately, God's perfectly arranged plans.

Cake That! by Heather Greer

Ten bakers. Nine days. One winner.

Competing on the *Cake That* baking show is a dream come true for
Livvy Miller, but debt on her cupcake truck and an expensive repair
make her question if it's one she should chase. Her best friend, Tabitha,
encourages Livvy to trust God to care for The Sugar Cube, win or lose.

Family is everything to Evan Jones. His parents always gave up their
dreams so their children could achieve theirs. Winning *Cake That* would
let him give back some of what they've sacrificed by allowing him to
give them the trip they've always talked about but could never afford.

As the contestants live and bake together, more than the competition
heats up. Livvy and Evan have a spark from the start, but they're in it to
win. Neither needs the distraction of romance. Unwanted attention
from Will, another competitor, complicates matters. Stir in strange
occurrences to the daily baking assignments, and everyone wonders if a
saboteur is in the mix.

With the distractions inside and outside the *Cake That* kitchen, will Livvy or Evan rise above the rest and claim the prize? Or does God have more in store for them than they first imagined?

Lightning Source UK Ltd.
Milton Keynes UK
UKHW021243160922
408971UK00009B/2020